Ghostly Lights

by Annick Hivert-Carthew

Illustrated by Martha Diebboll

Wilderness Adventure Books

ISBN: 0-923568-44-1

Story Illustrations by Martha Diebboll
Lighthouse Sketches by Erin Bardsley

Wilderness Adventure Books
P.O. Box 856
Manchester, MI 48158

Manufactured in the United States of America

Contents

Hope Island ◆ *Crazy Bugger* 1

South Haven ◆ *Things of the Past* 9

Selkirk ◆ *Shadows of Evil* 17

Lorain ◆ *A Corner of Heaven* 27

Marblehead ◆ *Choices* 37

Michigan City ◆ *The Catwalk* 43

Oswego West Pierhead ◆ *The Monument* 51

Grand Traverse ◆ *Need Help?* 59

St. Martin Island ◆ *Edward* 67

Manitou Island ◆ *Dead Calm Sea* 77

Old Presque Isle ◆ *Bluebeard* 85

Rock of Ages ◆ *The Painting* 95

Grosse Ile ◆ *Genuine Concern* 105

Crisp Point ◆ *It* 111

Nottawasaga Island ◆ *The Perfect Match* 113

Waugoshance ◆ *Matey* 121

Fort Gratiot ◆ *The Door* 129

Ile aux Galets ◆ *Friends* 133

Bete Grise ◆ *Shining Love* 141

Point Iroquois ◆ *Fred, Chuck, and Harry* 149

Lonely Island ◆ *Glorious Health* 155

Bibliography 160

Index 162

Featured Lighthouses

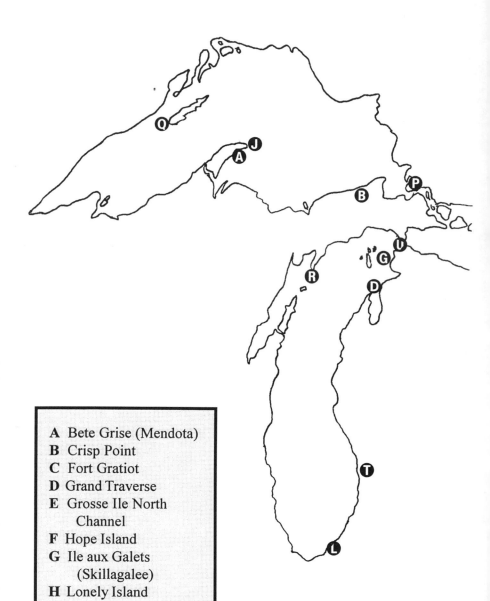

A Bete Grise (Mendota)
B Crisp Point
C Fort Gratiot
D Grand Traverse
E Grosse Ile North
     Channel
F Hope Island
G Ile aux Galets
     (Skillagalee)
H Lonely Island

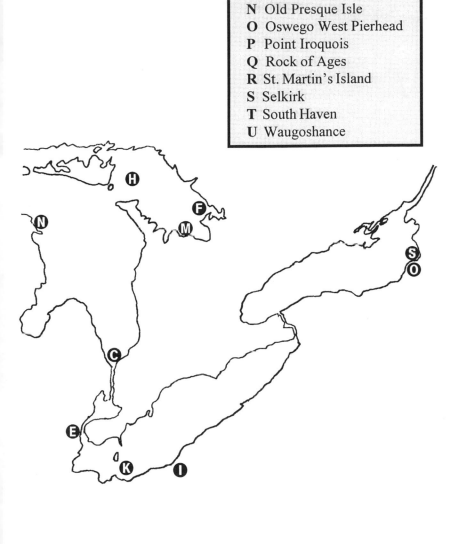

I Lorain
J Manitou Island
K Marblehead
L Michigan City
M Nottawasaga Island
N Old Presque Isle
O Oswego West Pierhead
P Point Iroquois
Q Rock of Ages
R St. Martin's Island
S Selkirk
T South Haven
U Waugoshance

Most people are fascinated by lighthouses, the first promise of land and shelter. They evoke nostalgia for a bygone era, when a solitary keeper struggled with not only the elements and other external dangers, but also loneliness and his or her internal demons.

Generally erected in the dramatic settings of the vast and dangerous Great Lakes, what structures could better appeal to our sense of adventure than these valiant sentinels flashing across a dark wilderness of water?

Today, lighthouses are beloved, but yarns of terror are even more popular. Most of us fall to the fascination of the supernatural, of being scared, of being chilled by ghost stories, literature of the strange and weird, of specters clanking their chains and seeking retribution.

Not every lighthouse has a ghost or a tale of terror. But trust an author's brain to create, to ride crests of horror, peaks of fear and stimulation, to pit readers against their worst terrors.

Imagine a remote lighthouse, madness, a roaring wind and foaming crests. You're on your own, trying to outwit an unknown and invisible evil . . .

With the exception of Harriet Colfax in "The Catwalk," the characters and plots are fictitious. I wish for these tales to inspire many of you to visit and support our beautiful lighthouses.

With deepest appreciation to:

A valued editor
Erin Sims Howarth, who took a chance on my first Cadillac book and edits my work with understanding and perception.

My husband, children, family and friends
Can you possibly read, listen to, or assist with the birth of another lighthouse story? Max, thanks for lugging camera equipment to countless lighthouses.

Everyone at Omega Productive Services, Inc.
My sincere gratitude for putting up with me, sharing computers, and patiently solving numerous never-before-seen technical problems.

The many people "of the Lakes" who have helped with this project.

Hope Island, 1920
Georgian Bay

Crazy Bugger

I'd been practicing midwifery in a little town in Georgian Bay for eight years when I was summoned to the bedside of old McTwain. He lived alone in a decrepit old house by the water, and was reputed to be terribly ill-tempered and strange. It was not the first time I was called to the bedside of the dying, for people often bestowed on the hands that brought them into this world the merciful grace to send them peacefully into the next.

McTwain was, in truth, a very peculiar old man. He had been keeper of the isolated lighthouse at Hope Island for ten years; but was so ancient that no one was old enough to recall his youth, and so disagreeable and repulsive that few dared address him. An inveterate drunkard, when bouts of ill-humor seized him, he turned into a dreadful fiend, spreading terror to those he met. Every one of his neighbors feared and loathed him. All avoided him.

I was not personally acquainted with this singular fellow, but had often seen his trembling figure stumbling pitifully about with the help of a strange carved cane that was said to have

1

landed several fatal blows. Children hung onto their mothers' skirts and voices dropped to a whisper at the sound of his name. Although a few bold youths crept up to his broken-down house to peer through the grimy panes, none dared taunt him or smash a window.

There were many aspects to his tottering gait, his rummy glazed eyes, that frightened old and young alike. Much was rumored about this gloomy individual. What was it, I often wondered, that provoked such terror and hostility in the hearts of otherwise friendly folks?

A day's worth of sailing away from the mainland, battered by the winds, Hope Island lighthouse had served mariners since 1884. Nestled amongst tall grass and beech trees, the light was said to be beautiful, and its white wooden tower and dwelling had always been a pleasant stop for many.

"Not always," warned the old ones, a look of terror on their deep-lined faces. "Not always."

"Beware of old McTwain," mumbled their pale lips.

"Murderer . . . Drunkard . . ." They murmured, furtively following his crooked back with fearful eyes.

Shivers coursed down my spine at the sight of the wretched man and my curiosity had long been piqued by his reputation in a way too shameful to admit to any living soul.

However, one night, a glass of sherry loosened my tongue and freed my inhibitions. I cunningly led the conversation to old McTwain's extraordinary case.

The story—or should I say rumor?—was never substantiated, but its essence was told to me by Mr. Martin, then the keeper at the light, after I had safely delivered Mrs. Martin of a healthy baby boy. The Martin family had returned to their winter quarters on the mainland just in time for the birth. While anxious neighbors pampered the new mother and child, the father and I shared a libation. My hands wrapped around a glass of sherry, I watched him sip on a snifter of brandy. All day the wind had howled but now, deep in the night, it shrieked in the chimney.

"Crazy bugger!" Martin said when the conversation turned to his infamous predecessor. "Never could get to the bottom of this business. As you know, I have fairly steady nerves, would never have got the job otherwise, but upon my word there is something disturbing at the light. Poke your head into the cellar and you'll feel it. A strange smell hangs about the place." His knitted brows and flustered expression showed that his thoughts had gone back to the light.

"Mean old man, got into trouble soon after taking his post, was summoned several times for ill behavior. It was way before my time. That summer, two fishermen, Ross and Graham, disappeared. Just disappeared. No trace." A visible tremor contorted the features of my host.

His peculiar manner increased my curiosity. Wetting my lips, I leaned forward. "You don't say!"

Trancelike, Martin continued. "McTwain had just been demoted. Took it badly. Some say he attempted to take his own life upon receiving the news." I gasped and lay back against the cushions, as though seeking comfort from their softness.

"By an appalling twist of fate, that same day a terrible storm developed and the two men, Ross and Graham, sought shelter at the light. Witnesses, other fishermen, saw their boat aiming straight for the island." His voice sank to a whisper. "No one ever saw them after that."

The glass shook in my hands. "What happened?" I cried.

He spoke quietly. I realized belatedly and with considerable embarrassment that to speak ill of one of his fellow keepers pained him greatly. I threw out my arms in a gesture of entreaty. "My dear Mr. Martin, you don't have to . . ."

Ignoring my plea, Martin continued. "We don't exactly know what happened. We can only assume that McTwain was in a terrible black mood, rambling in a drunken stupor, tottering about, gun pointed at his head. Horrified, the men pounced on him to pry the gun from his crazed hands. In his prime, the old man showed uncommon strength, and had assaulted the unwelcome visitors. Supposedly, he shot them and slashed their bodies to pieces."

I let out a breath I did not know I had been holding.

Sensing my agitation, he laid a hand on my trembling shoulders. "Come," he said, indicating the spirit case. "Another one?" Then he stood before the fire, and contemplatively gazed about the room.

"There was an investigation, you know. The whole place was turned upside down, dug up, shaken and scrutinized. Nothing!"

"What about the bodies? McTwain, the police?" I exclaimed.

Martin shrugged his shoulders. "Nothing came out of it. Bodies were never found, the crazy bugger never confessed. He was freed on lack of evidence."

I turned that over in my mind. "What about the strange smell in the cellar, the one you mentioned earlier?"

"Probably coming from the limestone walls." But Martin sighed with the air of a man who was far from content.

So, decades after the supposed deed, malicious gossip still brightened the wintry evenings of the townsfolk of Thunder Bay; but in this McTwain took no interest at all. Within me lay compassion for all suffering creatures. I pitied this solitary man whom the community shunned, and at whom cats spat and yowled savagely. Besides, my heart and mind were in my profession; there was a compelling Christian urge to attend to old McTwain's last breath.

In growing obscurity, his house stood with an unsettling air of loneliness, surrounded by gnarled trees and scruffy bushes. It had been left to decay for many years. Cracked bricks had tumbled amongst ragged weeds and into the path. Very nervously, I approached the ivy-clad sepulchral walls and ascended three slippery, moss-covered steps to push the door open, aware that no elderly woman, no man of the cloth had come to pray over the dying man.

It was locked. Surprised, I lifted the rusty iron knocker. After waiting uneasily for a considerable time in the depth of shadows beneath the decrepit porch, again I lifted the hammer and rapped it vigorously. The long wait in the obscurity made my heart thump in my chest.

Sensing a light scratchy tread inside the old place, I pressed one ear against the door. Slowly, feebly, yet heavily, the steps approached. There was a fumbling at the latch and the door grated inward.

I proceeded cautiously inside. No one was about. "Hello there!" Behind me the door creaked and slowly, ever so slowly, closed, blocking my last view of the outside world. Something brushed slightly against me, and it was gone. For a minute or two, I stood there, perturbed and unable to collect my thoughts; something had happened that I could not explain. My hands were icy cold.

I looked wildly around the room. The moonbeams shone weakly through a narrow window. In this ghostly light, old McTwain lay upon a bed, his cane resting next to him, one hand clutching it. How quiet! How pale! An old blanket lay tangled about his bony frame like a shroud. But it was not a corpse lying there; life pulsated in the room. I felt it with every hair, every pore of my skin—a strange, brooding life. My mouth was dry, as though filled with a bitter cloth of sadness; a faint rasping in McTwain's throat was the only sound disturbing the absolute silence.

My eyes fixed on the still figure, I crept toward the bed. A hoarse, half-choked shriek escaped my lips. His face convulsed with an indescribable terror, McTwain opened his eyes.

I was looking into the agony of a man waging the final battle for his soul with the devil himself. Again, something was gliding behind me. The fear that had gripped me a moment ago returned, but with renewed vigor. I shuddered violently.

A scream burst out of old McTwain. It was the bloodcurdling, tormented yell of a man plunging toward Hell. Blood throbbing in my ears, I moved to flee this loathsome house and its cursed occupant, but Old McTwain's gnarled, blue-veined hands clutched my coat with diabolical force. "You can't go! Save me! Save me! Ross! Graham! They're here! Here!"

His anguished voice sank to a whisper. "They're waiting, waiting . . . waiting," he babbled, and collapsed on his mattress in an exhausted heap.

Ross? Graham? The two men McTwain had allegedly murdered? How could I not remember this story? My heart nearly broke for pity, for loneliness, for suffering. At the gate of the hereafter, was McTwain being met by his victims?

Again I sensed a soft tread, and again felt the intrusion in the dark room of the invisible one. One whose appearance, I instinctively knew, is usually linked with death and grief. This is absurd, I reminded myself.

Trembling from head to foot, I retreated into the shadows of a huge armoire and slumped on a chair, awaiting the old man's last moment. The vigil was drawn-out and glum, so dismal I barely refrained from crying. Save for the chime of a distant church and McTwain's labored rasping, an oppressing silence had fallen upon the room.

Soon it was two o'clock.

The darkest hour.

In the pallid glow of the moon I saw it and my blood ceased to flow. The cane! The cane! It hovered above McTwain's head in a demonic dance. The old man, though in the throes of approaching death, felt its malevolence—he screamed hoarsely. The cane clattered to the floor, suddenly bereft of life, as though the cry had robbed it of all its strength.

A long stab of fear drove through my heart; I wanted to run out of the gloomy house and into the black cloak of the night. A low, pitiful rambling escaped McTwain's lips. Breathlessly, I crept back from the shadows and stood by the dying man. He caught me in a deathly grip and pulled me close to his ghastly breath. "I showed them." He began to sob quietly.

Showed them? Did he refer again to Ross and Graham? My brain reeled. Any trace of panic was drowned by vast curiosity. "Confess!" I cried. "Free your soul before it is too late. Did you kill Ross and Graham?"

Old McTwain writhed frightfully, eyes rolling, caught back, it seems, to the dreadful moment in the lighthouse when he had shot two men and horribly mangled their bodies in a fit of madness.

I leaned closer to his ear. "McTwain, did you do it?"

Under his bristling brows, McTwain's face was turning rigid.

Quickly! Quickly before death seals the whole mystery! "Where? Tell me, where are they?" I cried harshly.

A ghastly smile twisted his cracked and feverish lips. Slipping into Hell—the horror blazing in his eyes told me so—McTwain released his grip. "The . . . well," he gurgled, choking on putrid saliva. And at that moment he died.

In the shadow of a tattered curtain, the fickle moon showed me the dead face of old McTwain. From the corner of my eye, suddenly paralyzed with fear, I saw the cane resume its crazy dance. In one precise, whistling blow it crushed McTwain's brains.

Blood pounding in my ears, I wrenched open the door and staggered outside.

This story is based on John Hoar, Hope's third keeper (1891-1893), an ill-tempered man who allegedly murdered two fishermen who may have tried to stop him from committing suicide after he learned of his demotion. On his death bed, Hoar supposedly confessed to murdering the men and pitching them into a well he had built himself. An investigation took place. Inspectors carefully searched all the buildings. They dug everywhere. Nothing was found.

"Crazy Bugger" is how Achille Marchildon described John Hoar in an interview with a team of writers and photographers for the book *Alone in the Night* (Lynx Images, Canada, 1996). Mr. Marchildon, then 97, reported meeting John Hoar, and recalled Hoar's attempt to murder Achille's father at Hope Island lighthouse.

After being a landmark for mariners for over a hundred years, Hope Island lighthouse is now boarded up. In spite of the efforts of the local community and lighthouses enthusiasts, it has not been recommended for protection. Neglected and abandoned, over the years, it has fallen into the hands of vandals. Once a handsome, proud building, now some of its walls are crumbling, the stairs rotting, paint peeling, and its tower riddled with huge holes.

There is a strong movement to save Hope Lighthouse, and we want to believe it will succeed.

South Haven Light, 1995
Lake Michigan

Things of the Past

One hand on the door handle, the old lady hesitated. "Will you be okay, Dr. McKenzie?"

"Don't worry, Mrs. Hessan. I have much work to do."

Still, the kind old dear dithered, "You have my phone number in case you change your mind."

Thirty-five years old, I had hitchhiked across Europe, ridden wild horses across the Argentinian Pampa, chased poisonous snakes in India, taught Environmental History to hundreds of restless graduate students at a Big Ten University, and was paying alimony to two ex-husbands. Of course I'd be okay; a solitary night inside an ancient keeper's dwelling transformed into a museum seemed tame and safe.

I felt a heady rush of elation, a febrile anticipation at the idea of poring, undisturbed, over record books and documents, my favorite part of the job. The University had obtained for me the unique authorization to work days and nights (interrupted by as little sleep as possible) to search for missing documents on a particular Great Lakes keeper before dashing to Venezuela to deliver a paper three days hence.

"I'll lock the door behind you." A few reassuring words and a confident smile accomplished wonders.

Mrs. Hessan, a volunteer at the museum, who, in spite of her age, had stooped and bent and carried dusty boxes with unfailing courtesy and enthusiasm, relaxed a bit. "Remember, the guest room is ready." She departed after glancing at me one last time.

For the next three or four hours, I was busy. I worked diligently at a large rectangular table in the center of the room, bent over a litter of notes and manuscripts. Trevor Tavish had been an obsession of mine for over a decade. He had lost a leg during the Civil War and became keeper of South Haven light at the turn of the century. I was writing a biography but was still missing vital and elusive information. This trip was meant to fill in the gaps.

It was the beginning of summer; the sun sank quite late, and as it dipped a peaceful dimness invaded the dwelling. I delayed switching on the lights and ate my sandwich, gazing through the window at the light at the end of a long pier, blinking its brilliant eye across the darkening lake. Apart from tiny waves licking the shore, the jetty was quiet; the usual straggling fishermen and strollers had gone home to relax on their porches, relishing the lake's gentle breeze.

My eyes grew heavy and I think I crossed my arms on the table and lay my head down on it. I have no idea when or how long sleep claimed me, but I was wrenched from slumber by the stroke of midnight on the regulator.

A heavy and peculiar silence reigned within the obscurity of the room. My skin tingled with unease. "Don't be silly!" I said aloud and groped my way to a light switch. It clicked. Apart from a dry sharp noise, nothing happened. Darn it! Lost in unfamiliar surroundings, I ran my hands blindly along the walls in search of additional switches, cussing as knees and elbows bumped into chairs and other protruding furniture. Ah, there's one!

Click! No spark!

In sheer frustration, a nasty string of profanities escaped my lips. It did not improve the situation but relieved some of my mounting anxiety.

Telephone, go to the telephone, and call Mrs. Hessan. What number did she say? After another sightless jaunt across the room, my erring hands finally located it.

No tone.

"What does it mean?" I cried, voice shaking. The words bounced off the walls in a queer and disturbing self-repeating echo. Standing in the darkness of the museum, baffled, perspiration began to bead on my forehead.

At last the extraordinary noise stopped. I felt slightly faint and held my breath apprehensively.

Respite was only too brief. Scarcely had my chest relaxed when out of the walls, the ceiling, the wooden floor, even below the foundation itself, emanated a single wail, unbearably lonely, heartbreaking in its agony. When it finally melted into the darkness within, I was plastered against some bookshelves, shivering and panting erratically.

"Who's there?"

No reply.

After an anguished pause, "Who's there?" I screeched again, only faintly.

Suddenly the lights came on; the place resumed its usual coziness as if nothing had happened.

Not a stir to be seen, not a squeak to be heard.

I stood there, breathless, my back against the shelves, my hair on end, wondering if the whole affair had been an illusion, a post-sleep trance. Had my mind played a trick?

Shivering, incredibly disturbed, I toured the museum apprehensively looking for clues, knowing that answers would bring only anxiety. Either my imagination had worked overtime or the place was haunted.

Nothing was amiss.

An odd sense of being part of an unfathomable drama seeped into me. Nevertheless, I somehow managed to summon all that is stalwart in me to sit and resume work, peeping nervously now and then over my shoulder. Still burdened with a heavy foreboding, after a while, I managed to partly put the whole incident out of my mind, but the isolation of the house pressed upon me like heavy chains. Previously cherished silence became eerie, unbearable. An invisible menace, the premonition of some terrible calamity still filled a corner of my mind. Despairing of regaining my concentration and disgusted with myself, I flung my pen down and stared vacantly at the facing wall.

But recovering my senses was impossible, for at that precise moment all the lights dimmed slowly then died out.

I slumped in my chair, eyes roaming wildly in the terrible darkness within, hands and feet turning icy in spite of the sweat coursing down my back.

A keen wail of the same heart-splitting agony as before burst in the room. It echoed and reverberated around me. Soon it was joined by frantic voices, tens of people, men, women and children. Laments and cries of approaching death, of supplications, rang in my ears. "Help! Help! Over here!" "Take my child, oh, please save him!" "No, not without my husband!" "Goodbye, dearest love!"

Shock pinned my rigid body to the chair.

I was not alone.

Like an orchestra gone mad, each instrument battling for center stage, the voices increased their tempo, faster and faster, louder and louder. They went on yelling until the cacophony turned unbearable.

"Noooo!" I screamed, trembling fingers blocking my aching ears. I kept screaming, writhing with bitter anguish and pain, till I was hoarse with the effort. Then, inexplicably, the deafening utterances suddenly faded to a slight rumble.

A hiss, sharp and shrill, followed by a slight movement, a hardly discernible stir of air, passed by me. The next moment, it flowed, glacierlike, over me, ever so cold. A wild shriek, my own, pierced the gloom.

My mind, that strong ally who'd seen me through awful situations, after registering my near hysteria, took charge. Pull yourself together girl. Don't give in to panic. Think.

Shaky but with renewed strength, I batted furiously at the air around me, slicing through the night, striking at the invisible whatever, whoever. "Go away! Go away!"

With each blow, an icy blue mist clung to my skin, thicker and thicker. It grew heavier and tighter around my struggling form. Fueled by terror, my body put up its best fight, twisting and straining and stabbing at the abominable vapor that spat and swished over me. Exhausted, I stopped briefly to catch my breath. Sensing my ebbing strength, the thing rushed down my legs. It wrapped itself around my feet, climbed back up to my waist, pinned my arms to my sides and coiled around my chest with such demonic zeal that sobs of horror congealed in my throat. It dashed up my neck. I stiffened with fright. It was crawling up to my clenched mouth, up my nose! I'm going to die, entombed in the belly of a vile and alien cloud! My body shrank with unthinkable revulsion, unprepared for death by the unknown.

Oh, not to see the face of one's enemy!

A picture of my distraught parents and forlorn Nero, my beloved cat, of my smothered frozen body, flashed in my mind, just as the malevolent entity engulfed my head in one final voracious snap. "Aaaaaaah . . ."

It took me a few seconds to realize that I was not dead, that oxygen miraculously filled my lungs, that I could see.

A faint, yellow gleam was spreading throughout my tomb of blue ice. My eyes contracted under the sudden change, stared blankly at a strange picture developing quickly. Horribly misshapen creatures, concealed in black hooded cloaks cackled wickedly while gathering to form a gigantic wall. It undulated spasmodically, full of dark and intense suffering, quivering with the thunderous sound of crashing waves splintering wood with eternal fury. It appeared to recall a howling and tragic night on a treacherous reef, a gaping hole in a sinking ship, tormented bodies floating while others clung to bits of splintered wood or to each other. In the distance a lighthouse flashed its beacon. A bearded man in uniform battled the storm toward it, his small craft laden with sodden and terrified people. Here and there a terrible wail, a last gasp, a shriek, screeches of insanity, rode the foaming crests. One figure, a woman, clasped her arms around the lifeless body of a child, humming tragically into his ashen face while her own life was robbed by the raging waters. The world was a swirling terror. Dry, burning sobs welled within me, I tried to swallow and tried again.

A figure detached itself from the group. It burst into a ghastly peal of laughter as it raised a hand, the chalky outline of a dead face peeping from the shadows of its cover. At its signal all the creatures, as one body, pushed back their hoods. I gave a horrible cry. Their leathery skin was drawn tightly over protruding bones, lips twisted by death in a ghastly grin. Where once eyes gazed at sunrise now lay empty and sunken sockets. I was looking into the most revolting faces I had ever seen or imagined.

The loathsome demons lurched forward. I cringed and screeched with terror. Their leader snatched its cloak to smother my yells by wrapping it over my mouth, thin bony hands clenched like a vice. Then I think I fainted.

Maybe it was the tap-tap-tap on the floor, or the sudden agitation among the evil spirits that tore me from my daze. Anyhow, when I opened my eyes, the wall had disappeared, the abhorrent specters were slinking on the floor in abject servility.

Rat-ta-ta-tap.

Behind me and through the haze, I heard a door open. Help at last! Someone to chase my tormentors. My heart took on an accelerated beat.

The detestable fiends seemed instinctively to cling together.

I knew then that no human, but a greater power than they, had appeared.

Did the demons render me helpless for their master's use? Was the cloud quivering with my fear?

Tap-tap-tap.

Rooted in place, my enemies were visibly cringing.

I swallowed hard, but not hard enough to stifle an abject whimper.

The tap-tap-taps—footsteps, and not just footsteps—were getting closer. I strained to catch a glimpse of this new specter mighty enough to placate the devils at my feet.

It is often said that anticipation is worse than reality.

Then in the pallid light I saw him, an old cane clasped threateningly in one hand, his wooden leg tip-tapping on the floor. My brain was too agitated to notice more details.

All the creatures, including me, kept their eyes on him. Before I could guess his purpose, with a single leap of incredible agility, he sprang toward the beasts who recoiled and whined. He struck them haphazardly with the stick, roaring with uncontrolled rage. "You wretches! How could I save all of you! Too many! Too many! And me with a wooden leg!" Each shout was punctuated with a hissing strike, each ghostly figure vanishing one by one at its touch. "Go to your peace. Cease to torment me!"

At last, spent, the room emptied of cowering spirits, he leaned heavily on his cane.

Then, swivelling on his wooden leg, he turned to me, baton raised once more. At me. Petrified, mouth opened in a frozen cry, I gazed at him with unspeakable terror.

The stick plunged down.

With a whoosh, the cloud disappeared!

Instinctively, I jumped up and tottered like a drunkard as I walked, then crumpled in a heap onto the floor.

Tap-tap-tap.

The man—the phantom—leaned over me.

In spite of my fear, my eyes stared into his bearded face. The features before me were teasingly familiar. Who was he? I was certain to have seen him before. Where? How hard it is to think when one is afraid!

My eyes widened with recognition. Of course! I felt a stab of excitement that left me in complete wonder. The man who'd lost a leg in the Civil War and saved many shipwrecked lives—but not all of them—in spite of his wooden leg. Trevor Tavish, the man in the boat, keeper of this light. The man whose life was still much of a mystery to me.

"Mr. Tavish?"

Tavish's face broke into a crinkly smile. "Can I help you with your research?"

South Haven Light, first established in 1872, was rebuilt after the turn of the century. Its red steel tower and black parapet jut far into Lake Michigan, a dazzling sight against the turquoise waters. It is linked to the mainland by an elevated catwalk several hundred feet long, which enabled keepers to tend the beacon even in stormy weather.

The place and its gorgeous sunsets are a favorite with photographers and artists who hope to catch the light's regal silhouette against the blazing sky.

Its most famous keeper is James Donahue (1874-1909). Donahue fought in the Civil War, where he lost a leg. While stationed at South Haven, he saved many shipwrecked men despite his impediment.

Such a character is bound to attract the imagination of authors, but apart from being an inspiration for this story, we can be assured that Mr. Donahue is resting in well-earned peace.

Selkirk Light, 1842
Salmon River and Lake Ontario, New York

Shadows of Evil

It is said that terror strikes at night, but it seized Augustin Redon in the early morning during his daily walk. On that particular day, for no reason at all, except maybe absentmindedness due to anxiety, he took a slightly different route than usual. Behind a thick blanket of angry clouds, he knew a full moon had glowed through the night.

He knew, because he had heard her wails pierce shrilly through the storm. By now Gloria huddled in a corner, raving, gushing his name out with incredible loathing. Secretly, Augustin was afraid of his wife, he'd watched his back for a long time.

Hands stuffed deep in the pockets of his blue coat, he wandered about. A continuous gale had raged throughout the night, gigantic masses of foam had tortured the coast. It had played havoc with shipping traffic. Schooners, sails and rigging in a jumble, like some heaving, sinister shapes, had plowed across the leaping breakers of the storm. They blindly sought Augustin's yellow blinking light at the entrance of the Salmon River, their refuge on the fickle and turbulent waters of Lake Ontario.

Augustin had tended the light and its eight hungry mineral oil lamps with unfailing devotion. After such a night, most keepers would have gone straight to sleep, but not Augustin. The Frenchman was trying to calm the banging of his heart.

That morning, as every morning following a full moon, he feared facing his demented wife. Gloria Redon, a beak-nosed Englishwoman of a peculiar pallor, had always likened sex to boiled cabbage and served them both tepid.

Except on full moons.

How Augustin had come to loath this peculiar twilight, when darkness and light tangled for dominion over land and water, and he fought his own demon!

Once a month at midnight, an ominous, raspy panting jolted Augustin out of his sleep. Then, and only then, flannel gown hitched up to the navel, an odd agitation, less sexual than coming from a mysterious, repellent need within, shook Gloria's withered body. His wife's features twisted horribly, mouth gaping, eyes protruding in a revolting way. A wild and terrible struggle, a nightmare ensued.

Clawed at, bitten, held in a vise by scrawny legs of unsuspected strength, trying to control his revulsion, Augustin—an energetic, burly man—piteously parried each repugnant assault. Some unexplainable and uncontrollable weakness invariably dissolved his vigor. The disheveled and keening creature seemed to possess an uncanny force. Strident laughter echoed in his ears; she rode him cruelly as a witch would ride her steed. Once, she broke two ribs and jarred his neck.

At fifty-seven, he'd suffered ten years of this monthly and peculiar abuse. For the past two years, always carefully for he felt danger closing in, Augustin had contrived to avoid the marital bed, especially on full moons, when her abominable howling tore through the night. Two years ago, that's when he met sweet, soft Alaina of the long blond hair, his lady love.

That's when Gloria's disturbing gaze began to carefully follow his every move. That's when a feeling of anguish as he had never experienced before first pounded in his chest.

The customary walk at sunrise, free of the worries and demands of wife and light, unchained his spirit; the moment belonged to him, and to him only.

When he became aware of a strange purplish light surrounding him and a flurry of dark motion among the maple trees, he slowed, gazing around him. He heard something swish. A flight of ravens appeared in the air, screeching madly, a hellish sort of cry combined with taunting peals of exultation.

Augustin stared, fascinated. In confusion his brain recorded the singularly long and grotesque claws, the demonic shine in the beady eyes. One bird in particular, a repellent, monstrous beast, twice as large as the others, was looking at him intensely. It swooped inches from his head. Startled, Augustin ducked. His first reaction was disbelief. The raven cackled mockingly as it took another swipe at him. Baffled and anxious, wondering if his tired mind was playing tricks, Augustin began to perspire profusely. Was the bird actually attacking him? And were the other creatures really screeching a kind of devilish cheer? His heart began to race—he sensed the presence of danger.

The beast flew closer, twisted claws reaching for its prey's hair. Augustin leaped back. Not quickly enough. He felt a ripping, a searing pain. Something warm began to trickle down his neck. The raven soared amongst its clamoring flock in a triumphant lift, a piece of ragged skin and a tuft of hair in its grasp.

When he could think again, Augustin tore off his coat and flailed arms and garment around him. A wild, hoarse yell burst from his lips.

In a discordant twitter, the flock made to descend, but their leader shrieked sharply. Suddenly subdued, as one body, the birds settled on nearby branches, feathers quivering with repressed excitement.

A strange anticipation seemed to possess them.

All unblinking eyes were fixed on the Frenchman with obscene hunger. The gigantic raven emitted another demoniac screech. Augustin shuddered—dread crept into his chest. Then, with growing fright, he saw the world he thought he knew go mad around him.

As if spurred by some dark, unseen power, in a horrible burst of squawking, the birds began to circle and dive around his frightened figure. Too late, Augustin understood this to be a hideous dance of death. Acute terror welled up within him.

Led by the monstrous raven, the accursed flock hurled itself at him. The birds clawed furiously and pecked and picked and tore; a reddish froth flew from their voracious beaks.

Smothered by a vicious black cloud, terror piling on terror, Augustin sucked in air and staggered, body writhing in pain. In his fight with death, he frantically shielded his eyes and face with his hands. His scalp lacerated to a bloody mess, crimson rivulets coursed between his torn fingers; several nails were ripped off and one thumb hung in shreds.

Screams bubbled in his throat, but frozen with horror, the outcry congealed. He twisted in despair, fell to the ground and scrambled weakly for footing in a chaos of feathers, beaks and claws. He heard again the hellish alien screeches, sensed a growing excitement, a new energy in the murderous flock.

They knew, as he did, blood gushing out of his mouth, that the end was near. Soon, they would feed undisturbed, picking at his flesh, leaving his bones to wild dogs.

The loathsome mass of flapping black wings knocked him down. He crumpled on a bed of crackling leaves, all the fight gone out of him. Pictures of his gabled stone lighthouse, of ships floundering in the night, flashed in his mind.

Unbeknownst to Augustin, he had stumbled across some appalling ancient rite. It heralded the approach of more shocking horrors than he could have ever imagined.

The purplish light turned phosphorescent. A humming sound, very much like rhythmic chant, droned over the place. The vermin suddenly fell into a reverent sort of hush; they stopped their assault, and heads bowed low, hurriedly formed a guard around the fallen man. Augustin heard a clear, sweet voice emerging from the woods. The great beast's wings deployed in an imposing lift.

At that instant, a sensuously shaped young woman emerged from the shadows, her only garment, a band of rainbow across her forehead. Hips undulating, breasts swaying gently with each step, she raised a graceful hand. The raven gently settled on it.

Releasing the beast, the maiden sank down next to the keeper. He had an instant of ecstatic fear immediately followed by a powerful rush of lust he had not felt since his youth, not even with Alaina. Her face was thin and pale, so very pale, almost ethereal and yet incredibly beautiful. The hooked nose was oddly familiar; he made a befuddled effort to identify it. Unnaturally transparent lids and thick lashes partly concealed huge shrewd eyes of a ghostly shade. Her hands, swifter than butterfly wings, fluttered over Augustin. Their touch was cool, almost icy. At their contact, he felt a great healing power surge through him; the pain disappeared, one by one his wounds vanished. A new thumb sprouted over the injured one. This magical, singular skill should have awakened caution and wonder, but overwhelming desire impeded logic.

A corner of his brain warned that her hands were sallow and more spidery than graceful, but all the same, he was enraptured. His heart took on a furious beat, passion increased. Their eyes met. She pulled him to his feet with no apparent effort and led the way to a path of unearthly hue that he could have sworn had not existed before.

Regardless, like a moth to a flame, incapable to resist, he followed her into the infinite depth of the unknown, and hence straight into the shadows of evil.

The alien chant grew louder; peculiar sounds, many voices pulsated to the rhythmic beat of a drum. Augustin experienced a distinct feeling of entering a bizarre hidden world; he glanced nervously over his shoulder. A tangle of gnarled trees stood where the path should have been. As if sensing his concern, the maiden spun around to place glacial, tormenting lips over his open mouth. The chill blistered his skin, jerked his nerves; he made to flee. Fingers crawled, spiderlike, up the hapless man's back and coiled around his neck with exceptional force. Hypnotic dark eyes fixed upon fearful ones, gripped their gaze and held fast, inexorably drawing him toward destiny.

They emerged in a field slopping gently into a valley. At first Augustin was blinded by the radiant light. In front of him, the maiden grew thinner and lost her voluptuous contours. In a wild leap, she pounced back, letting out a bloodcurdling whoop.

Augustin gave a horrible cry.

Gone were the beautiful features, the luscious body; blue-veined skin dangled loosely over cadaverous limbs; breasts once rounded and tantalizing were shriveled and sagging; and the face, contorted with hatred, was Gloria's, only more hideous! He regarded her with uncomprehending revulsion. Bloodshot eyes glowed grotesquely from inky sockets. The mouth, a toothless and distorted black hole, was drooling. It spat a vindictive curse. The band of rainbow, the only reminder of her ephemeral beauty, still glistened on Gloria's forehead.

In one swift move, the repulsive woman snatched it off. It sailed through the air to snap around Augustin's chest and arms faster than a whip and stronger than manacles. The wretched man's cry turned into a frightful scream.

With a harsh, exultant laugh, Gloria—could that malevolent creature really be his wife?—prodded him forward with rawboned fingers. He shuddered uncontrollably.

Just as a wave of nausea convulsed his insides, the field burst into a dreadful clamor. A multitude of women, their gaunt and nude bodies bedaubed with bright paints, scurried from the valley, brandishing sticks and knives, screeching and yelling. As they approached, Augustin, sick with apprehension, noticed the revolting sadistic countenance, the glinting eyes, similar to Gloria's. A tall, ghostlike woman marched ahead, resplendent yet macabre in a flowing robe, a crimson shroud hanging slack over one shoulder. Behind the priestess, for it had to be a sort of priestess—her bearing was regal in spite of the grisly eyes—a blond woman was dragged, clothes in tatters, the witches goading her with incandescent sticks.

The woman's sweet heart-shaped face, smeared with ashes, came into view.

"Alaina, my love!" moaned Augustin in astonishment. How? This must be a hallucination, a horrible nightmare. Like a stalked

animal, she turned bruised, frightened eyes on him. He writhed and twisted, a beastly roar dying upon his lips.

The haggard captive was maliciously kicked forward. She sprawled like a broken puppet. "Alaina!" he shouted, agony in his voice.

Gloria's fiendish laughter cut in on his torment.

The priestess raised an imperious hand. "State the crime," she said to his wife.

"Treachery and neglect," she replied.

"What is your wish?"

Gloria's repugnant form exuded hatred. "Vengeance! Eternal death."

The ghastly witches jostled and crowded by a nearby tree. "Kill! Kill! Kill!" they chanted viciously, shaking with the onset of murder-madness, bodies and limbs contorted in a series of eerie motions that could only have been created by a sorcerer from the pit of Hell.

"Augustin, run from this evil place! Save yourself!" Alaina cried frantically, her gaze filmed with terror.

Before he knew what happened, a swift invisible force hurled her to the tree and pegged her against its trunk.

Petrified, Augustin saw a sinister fever animate the witches' repellent shapes. All the creatures pointed at him with despicable expectation. What new terror were they scheming?

Something shockingly cold slammed over his mouth.

The horrendous thought that he was to witness death came to his mind. A new terror gripped him. As he opened his mouth to shout, the cold thing slipped between his teeth to fill the whole cavity. It muffled his cries.

The priestess brutally struck the hostage across the face. A violent stab of pain, flowing strangely from Alaina to him, knocked his head backward. A surge of terror coursed in his veins. A vague notion of deviltry crept in his mind, but everything that was sane in him rejected it.

The crowd gave a jubilant thrill. Alaina looked at him in misery.

The vile sorceresses leaped on their victim with knives and

sticks. Alaina screamed agonizingly again and again. Gasping for breath, Augustin suffered each blow, every strike contorted him as it did the woman. The appalling significance of this mysterious occurrence suddenly hit him. In a diabolical manner, Alaina and he were sacrificed to Gloria's fiendish revenge. Both were victims, her pain had become his. It was horrible. They endured torture he did not believe humans were capable of surviving. Would it ever end?

In minutes, Alaina was reduced to a whimpering, incoherent, bleeding figure covered with terrible gaping wounds. At last, she sunk into unconsciousness and died.

Augustin expired two minutes later.

He awoke to the mad screeching of ravens with long and grotesque claws above his head. One bird in particular, a repellent monstrous beast, was looking at him intensely. The gigantic raven emitted a demoniac screech. Augustin shuddered, a sudden dread crept in his chest. He saw the world he knew go mad around him.

As if spurred by some dark, unseen power, the birds hurled themselves at him, clawing and pecking and tearing . . .

Forever trapped in hell, Augustin had stumbled into eternal death.

Built in 1838 at the mouth of the Salmon River on Lake Ontario, Selkirk Light is one of the most historic buildings on the Great Lakes. It was probably named after Thomas Douglas, Earl of Selkirk, who purchased vast areas of land on the Salmon River in the late 1790's and became very wealthy in subsequent real estate deals,

In 1615 Samuel de Champlain and the Hurons marched through the site of the future lighthouse; in 1684, a treaty between Iroquois tribes and French Governor-General de la Barre was signed there; and it turned into a refuge for smugglers during the war of 1812.

The first permanent settlers came in the early 1800's to harvest the bountiful Atlantic Salmon that spawned there every year. The fishing and shipbuilding industries soon boomed. The light was erected to protect the numerous ships stopping for business around Selkirk. It was taken out of service twenty years later, when local trade began to dwindle.

The lighthouse, a beautiful gabled fieldstone dwelling, is being restored by its owners and is available for rent as daily, weekly or monthly accommodation.

Lorain Light, 1965
Lake Erie, Lorain, Ohio

A Corner of Heaven

You may not know this, but there is a corner of heaven reserved for lighthouse keepers.

A special corner for special keepers.

An azure sky blazing on emerald waters slightly ruffled by a cooling breeze; a light blinking brilliantly without constant refilling and cleaning save a caress of wizened hands for old times sake; men and women rocking contentedly in the shade of an ancient dwelling.

Many aspire to its entrance, the ultimate eternal reward.

To be admitted one has to present an impeachable record at the gates.

A few are denied access on a mere skillet left on a stove, laundry hanging on the wrong day or left on the line too long.

Once, such were the demands of the Great Establishment in its pursuit of perfection and regularity. It had devised an instruction book—The Book—which, in long and somber paragraphs, organized all aspects of the lives of its most faithful servants. Words such as unfailing devotion, duty-bound, immaculate conditions, constantly alert, and irreproachable character, were mentioned more times than one brushed teeth.

Transgression provoked severe reproof, a black mark as ugly and monstrous as a cuckoo in a robin's nest. A zealous troop of inspectors "dropped by," unannounced, to ensure the enforcement of implacable rules.

For those of you who wonder if such perfect creatures, keepers without a single violation, ever existed, the answer is yes.

Many.

Men and women.

Where did the others go?

Fortunately, rules of the above, devised by a higher being, are more sympathetic to sinners than their earthly associates.

One chance. Those with an occasional flaw got one chance at redemption.

For ten years they had to guard an assigned tower against all mishaps; no mechanical defects, damaging storms, sinking ships, loss of lives. Nothing. Of course, only the light acknowledged their presence; humans might have sensed it but never saw it.

One slight mistake and the guardian angels were "out," zapped pronto up to "common" heaven where no beacon would shine endlessly in their souls.

The particular keeper I have in mind, one named Geff Roberts, died in 1944 while rescuing ten shipwrecked men. Alas, the gates of Keepers' Corner banged shut upon his arrival. His crime: he had once left a dirty plate on the kitchen table. Though he defended his cause with passionate energy (Mr. Roberts was having dinner at the time of an emergency call), he still required redemption. He was serving time for this grave error of judgment, and was nine months away from deliverance when this story begins.

Nine more months—that's what was left of his sentence. It had been a cushy job. Everybody loved the light, seamen, captains, keepers, and the good people of Lorain. Even the Army

Corps of Engineers had taken special care designing and building it. A homey appearance, a pitched roof and shutters, belied its strength. A bomb-shelterlike structure of steel and concrete, it was meant to last and endure Lake Erie's infamous storms.

Roberts sighed with contentment.

Present keeper Bruce was efficient and smart; had listened to his telepathic advice without knowing it and had ignored the book for the most part, paying strict attention only to operation, safety and navigation rules. Nice guy.

It was a happy time.

Ten o'clock. Bruce should come to bed soon.

At first, new at the job of ghosting and nervous about his charge, Geff had spent the night in the keeper's chamber—not in the same bed, no, no, devotion to duty did not go that far, even The Book did not insist upon it. He'd watched over Bruce, standing in a shadowy corner of the room (spirits can sleep in any position they like). As a good guardian, he had sent over pleasant dreams—too pleasant; the man's happy snores rumbled like cannons in the dwelling, giving Geff a mighty headache. He had tried adjusting the sweetness of the keeper's reverie.

To no avail.

Bleary-eyed, (ghosts need rest, too) Geff had peeled his invisible form from the wall, glided to a nearby room and had slept there ever since.

There he was, that particular night, on the second floor of the old house, when the telephone rang. Bruce was just going up to bed, Geff heard a mild oath and retreating steps.

"Allo. What? . . . When? . . . I see . . ."

Usually he did not pay much attention to telephone talk, mostly routine calls. Lately, the smoothness of the job had made him a bit indolent, but this time the tone of the conversation caught his ear.

There was a definite edge of quiet desperation in the voice.

Geff did not bother with the stairs; he flew straight through the ceiling.

His ward was staggering to a seat and sunk into it, a gloomy and sad expression etched on his face. That's when Geff squeezed into the wire to listen.

"When did you say again? Why?"

"In two weeks. That's when the new beacon will be operational."

"What will happen to this one?"

"It will be decommissioned and demolished soon after, give or take ten days."

"They'd promised me to keep it . . ."

"You can understand that the Coast Guard cannot afford to keep two lights going."

"I see . . ."

"The new one will be fully automated, cheaper to run."

Bruce flung out his hand, the victim of a rising tide of helplessness. Who, after all, could be brave enough to take on the Great Establishment?

Now, it was Geff's turn to shiver with horror. His chance to Keepers' paradise plummeting in the shovels of demolition crews! The appalling threat benumbed his brain.

He scooted out of the wire to drag himself to a chair.

Sad and weary, Bruce slumped on his seat.

One man and a specter drooped opposite one another with identical expressions of desperate and ardent longing.

There followed a silence about the house, which told what was passing in the two "men's" minds; in two weeks their respective lives would be drastically altered.

For thirty minutes the gloomy spell lasted, then it was broken by the strident peal of the telephone. Startled, Bruce glared at it as if it had grown horns. One hand hesitatingly stretched toward it. A loud voice boomed in the receiver.

"Bruce? Marcus here. 'Thought I'd give you a call. Just heard the news from Ben. Sorry about that, old chap. We had a drink together, told me he got a contract to demolish the light, doesn't really want to do it. People here aren't going to like it."

"I don't like it either."

"Shame really . . ."

"Yeah . . ."

Geff had invaded the line again. Old Marcus, Old Faithful! Marcus was attracted to the light like a bee to honey. Why hadn't Geff thought of him? Of course! Flash. Action. Come on, Marcus, old boy, say it.

"Eh, Bruce, I was just thinking. Couldn't we organize a committee? A petition? 'Save the Light' sort of thing?"

A little gleam of hope shone briefly in Bruce's eyes. It dimmed quickly. "What? In two weeks?" he said, balefully.

Geff got agitated. Blast! I can't do the job alone. You've got to help me, guys.

Bruce looked at the wire, twisting erratically, and dreamily slapped it.

Ouch!

"I'll make a few calls, we'll be in touch tomorrow morning. Who knows . . ."

"Thanks Marcus."

Geff did not sleep one wink. He worked all night. It was obvious these guys needed more time. How?

For the next ten days, mind restless, heart too full, he lay silent and motionless for the most part, thinking, cogitating, imagining wild schemes to save the light, none of which, he knew, would work. Marcus called daily, frantically recruiting help and support for the "Save the Light" project. Enthusiasts spoke out, recruited signatures, squeezed purses, wrote arousing articles, and generally awakened people's outrage at the possibility of losing a beloved landmark. Since most humans dislike having something taken away from them, the closer it got to the fatal date, the more cherished the light became. Folks who had not cared a straw before now grumbled bitterly. A steady group of supporters picketed on the shore, their voices forcefully haranguing citizens to call friends and relatives in power to reverse the Coast Guard's decision. Bright placards invited the population to write to Congress. But more time, more people, and more money were needed. The usual.

Short of a miracle, the light was doomed—and so was its guardian angel.

On the eleventh day, a drizzly morning, Geff still had not come up with a solution. The voices outside were getting more desperate. He got up to watch the beacon flash for the first time at the end of its brand new breakwater. Only a few stragglers had braved the weather to attend the official opening.

That same evening Bruce quietly turned his blinker off. After almost fifty years of shining upon the Lake, the tower was swallowed by the night, its lonely structure silhouetted against a starry sky.

The next day, Bruce packed his bag, bundled reports and journals in boxes and took one last tour of his domain, eyes lingering sadly on empty spaces and bare walls. He turned off all the lights, switched off the heating, stepped out and bolted the door behind him.

It was ten o'clock at night.

Bereft and lonely, Geff dragged himself to the nearest corner to indulge in a fit of self-pity.

Two minutes later there was a fumble at the door. It creaked open. Bruce walked in clumsily with the air of a man with an embarrassing matter on his mind. He cleared his throat and shuffled on his feet. "Well, er, . . . forgot to say goodbye," he muttered almost shyly in the darkness within. "Er, thanks . . . whoever you are," and left.

No, no, no, the mist over Geff's eyes could not be tears. Angels don't cry.

An empty house, an October chill preparing earth and water for bitter frost; a ghost so drained and forlorn as he rested against a wall in a dwelling that seemed a grave. Could he settle for an afterlife in regular heaven? One for folks fond of rich soil and green spaces, when all he cared about was shimmering waters and flashing lights?

On day thirteen, machines arrived at the shore nearby. "See you tomorrow," shouted a foreman to the machinists.

Tomorrow. A wild anxiety chewed in Geff's stomach. Time had almost run out, yet giving up was unacceptable.

It was at midnight that night when, in the most abject depth of despair, spurred by his own indomitable energy and resourcefulness, the wildest idea flashed in his mind. Yes. Yes. It could work. He'd never done it before, never stretched his powers that far. It would be exhausting and would require men of strong mettle.

Let's see. Jim, his old buddy, was serving time in Toledo light. Geff sat cross-legged in the center of the room to meditate hard and deep to increase his telepathic ability. First, expel negative ideas, stretch and elongate powers, reach, reach, reach. His mind remained anchored in its ethereal body.

Geff labored and strained, shivering with the effort, with frustration. Tremor after tremor passed through his suffering shape, so much so he feared he'd burst into smithereens.

Then it slowly came; a feeling of emptiness and yet intense wholeness, an amazing blend of forces, of concentrated vitality, unspoken words communicating as clear as a bell. "Hey, Jim, is that you?"

"Geff . . . Geff!" No mistaking the surprised and warm ebullience in the voice.

"Listen, I don't have much time. I really need your help."

"Shoot, buddy."

In brief sentences, Geff outlined his plan.

"I think it could be done, but it will require more than just the two of us."

"I know. 'Thought of Brian at Cleveland, Frank at Fairport, and Dan at Buffalo Main."

"Frank and Dan will do it, but Brian is gone."

"To Keepers' Corner?"

"Yeah. Lucky dog. Do you know Bob at Erie Land, in Pennsylvania?"

"No. Do you?"

"He's a good guy; we went to school together. I'll reach him for you."

"Thanks. Any news of Jon at Vermillion?"

"He'll do it, needs a redeeming point, has the Almighty on his tail; he almost lost a sailboat yesterday."

"I just remembered Phil at Dunkirk; met him at the gates. We were refused access at the same time."

"When do we start?"

"Tomorrow, before dawn, six o'clock; it'll take some time to pull forces. Remember: all at once, the whole day, rest at night."

"Do you think we can maintain that 'til winter?"

"Just pray for an early one."

The next morning was pretty frisky; a frigid wind blew vigorously from the northeast, from New York, Pennsylvania and northern Ohio. It boldly whipped the faces of protesters and friends gathered to snap last pictures or simply hold hands. Old Ben and his workers atop their machines were all muffled up.

Ben signaled, motors burst into snores amid a heavy silence from the crowd. Several women bore traces of tears upon their cheeks.

Inside the ancient light, Geff was profoundly focusing on his internal being, a blue glaze of intense concentration coursing through his taut form. Energy, more and more, and more. Outside, the wind whistled against the tower, calling and calling. The guys from Buffalo, Dunkirk, Erie Land and Fairport had arrived.

It began as a swirl nipping at the foundation, flirting tentatively with the breeze, then, growing bold, taking strength and exuberant pleasure at their union. It was soon joined by Brian from Cleveland and Jon from Vermilion. It exploded into a foaming, booming chasm of mountainous dimensions, spitting and thundering over the breakwater. House, tower, land and water had commingled into a gray, howling mass.

It had come so quickly, from so many directions, there was a confused stir among the spectators. Rubbing his wet face, Ben peered at the angry crests and shook his head. "Can't do it today," he said. He and crew slunk away under jubilant cheers.

For thirty days, Geff and his mates sustained the fury of the elements. They dashed back at night, weak with fatigue, to their respective lights and crumbled in exhausted heaps within their walls.

Meanwhile, the "Save the Light" movement interpreted this wondrous reprieve as a blessing of God. They gathered momentum and worked furiously, diligently at raising funds, collecting signatures, and generally hounding Congress and several state representatives.

For thirty days Ben and his crew took their positions, got drenched and whipped, shook their heads and left.

Now and then, the squall lost some of its bite as if exhausted. Its erratic and searing panting was very much like a runner's breath after the final spurt of speed over the finish line, except that this storm was not yet finished and saved its energy for the last stupendous dash.

At last, winter decided to combine impetus. Frost, sleet and snow began to ride the storm. Shaking their heads for one last time, Ben and his crew retreated for the season.

The good people of Lorain shouted with joy, champagne flowed at parties. An amazing miracle had been wrought upon them; they now had time to raise funds and lobby Congress.

The light was saved from destruction.

Geff's task at last was done.

Early June of the next year, he went straight to Keepers' Corner, where he's been telling his story ever since.

As told in this story, Lorrain Light was built in 1917; its quaint town home appearance, with pitched roof and wooden shutters, became a landmark for many captains. Built like a fortress, it could withstand the worst of Lake Erie's battering storms.

The Coast Guard decided to decommission and demolish it in 1965 in favor of a new automated beacon they had built at the end of a recently constructed breakwater. However, they overlooked the affection the community bore their light.

Concerned citizens formed a committee to save the structure, but would have run out of time if it had not been for providential storms thundering over the lake, delaying the wrecking operation. When the storms finally calmed down, winter had set in. The light was saved from destruction.

Today, although out of service, it has become the symbol of Lorain and is celebrated all over town. To the delight of enthusiasts, murals, napkins, glasses, calendars—everything in the community—pays tribute to its enduring light.

All's well that ends well in Lorain.

Marblehead Light, 1998
Lake Erie, Bay Point, Ohio

Choices

"Aaaah!"

Jack had climaxed.

Jack was great at noises, not so good at foreplay.

From beginning to end the whole interlude did not last long enough to spell my name—a short one: Morgan Field.

My boyfriend, no, ex-boyfriend—Jack was definitely out in more ways than one (and I could not tell the difference, that's how bad it was)—collapsed on my shoulder with a gratified sigh, which was more than I could say.

That's when I saw him—the other man—watching us in the blinking incandescence of the light, leaning nonchalantly against the whitewashed tower. He stood barely fifteen feet from us, puffing on a small cigar with a pungent smell.

Startled, mortified, I shrieked thinly.

"It was good for you too . . ." muttered Jack against my neck.

I tried to wriggle free of his white body and groped for the blanket spread underneath us. "Jack, don't be stupid! Get up! Someone is watching us!"

His head lifted quickly. "Where?"

"There, by the tower."

"I can't see anything."

"Come on, have a better look. He is just a few feet away." The stranger's dark-clad form stood clearly against the white stones. He was wearing some sort of uniform and his eyes rested on me. I could not quite see them, but felt their touch on my exposed skin.

"There's nothing there."

"Look, he is smoking, can't you see the red glow of his cigar? Smell it?" The creepy man stood there, blowing smoke and staring at me.

"Are you joking?" No mistaking the annoyance in Jack's voice.

Anger exploded in my chest. "A filthy voyeur is upon us and you're not doing anything." Disgusted, my hands pushed him off roughly. Jack was a complete wimp. "I'm going to give him a piece of my mind, if you won't."

In a rage, I rose, grabbed the blanket and decanted my date on the hard stony ground, aware of a distant glare following my every move, branding my naked flesh with its intensity.

My hands clumsily wrapped the woolen fabric around my body, one corner flung over my shoulder like a peplos. Fueled by increasing fury, I marched toward the intruder, shouting and gesticulating. "Dirty, rotten bastard! I'm going to call the police!"

Two or three feet away, the stranger smiled, one eyebrow cocked arrogantly.

"Morgan, come back. Calm down, there's nobody there!" Jack had slipped on his jeans and captured my arms from behind. "Look, nobody." His hand swept the air, slashed across and through the distinct figure standing close to us, exhaling little clouds of cottony smoke against the ghostly whiteness of the structure. "Nothing!"

Considerably perturbed, I turned to Jack.

His impatient and patronizing look told me he did not see anything unusual.

"But . . ." I began. The man slowly shook his head and raised a warning finger to his lips. Suddenly unsure, I tried to control the trembling of my knees and the banging of my heart. A frightening thought, too bizarre, too fantastic to believe, poked in a corner of my mind. I stood riveted to the ground, momentarily paralyzed, questioning my sanity.

Jack was still holding me. "Let me go!" I screeched, squirming to break free. I stretched a hesitating hand toward the apparition—what else could I call it? Suddenly a gust spiraled between us. His image faded in a purplish cloud, but not before I noticed the well-trimmed, light beard and longish curly hair underneath the visor of a battered cap similar to those of the Confederate soldiers. A ghostly blur drifted silently past. When the swirling haze settled, he was gone. I emitted a shrill wail, as if abruptly bereft of I did not quite know what; an inexplicable and terrible feeling of hollowness, of sadness washed over me.

Jack and I finished dressing in silence. Just as I was folding the blanket, a voice, deep and vibrant, murmured throatily in my ears. "Good night Morgan."

I spun around, holding my breath. The man or his shadow had appeared again by my side. He was tall and lithe, a faint aroma of tobacco and saddle soap hung about him, not unpleasant at all. His gaze, intense and enticing, lingered on my face, slowly descended down my throat, and settled there, just where blood pulsated erratically in my veins. It dispersed a shiver of excitement, awoke a disturbing awareness of my body I could not quell and did not try to. The whole experience was irrational, disconcerting, yet irresistibly fascinating. Increasingly aware of the mounting tension between us, my mouth went dry. Standing this close, my will crumbled, overwhelmed by the power, the unyielding energy in him. Our gazes locked. "Come back tomorrow, I shall be waiting for you," he said quietly. His voice carried a distinct southern drawl filled with thrilling promise.

Almost against my will, I knew I would return.

Jack and I walked to the car as strangers; a vision, a specter separated us; the experience had catapulted me to a world of illusions, of ifs and self-questioning.

The following night, the wind chopped about, waves dashed against the solid rock, their crests carrying the distant wind-borne notes of my name.

I found him at the foot of the light, smoking another cigar. Catching sight of me, he peeled himself off the wall to ground the stub with a booted foot and beckoned me with a lazy gesture of his wrist.

Apprehensive yet helpless, I crossed the distance separating us as if in a dream. He wore gray, a uniform of long, long, ago. A foot apart, we looked deep into each other's eyes, searching, reaching for each other's inner being. For several minutes we did not speak. Again, a sensual thrill vibrated within me. That I was falling under the spell of a power greater than I understood entered my mind, but danger captured my senses. I was afraid yet unable to resist.

"What's your name?"

"Jordan Winstate, at your service, ma'am." He bent gallantly at the waist.

"What do you want from me?" I whispered breathlessly.

Gently, he caught hold of one of my fluttering hands and brought it to his mouth for a kiss. Then, wetting a finger tip, he ran it across my parted lips and let it slowly trail down to the top of my heaving bosom. And lower still. Without a word, he drew me into his arms. My fear was intense but the warmth emanating from his body felt real, not icy or chilly as Gothic novels usually describe. It was searing with desire, human desire, a strange powerful force. Scarcely knowing what was happening, body instantly soft and pliant, weak with longing, I pitched even closer.

"Ah, should you ask?" He said, tipping my chin upward. "A cure for loneliness, of course."

And he kissed me. It was more than a kiss, it was a branding—burning, irresistibly passionate.

"Why me? Why?"

"You're the chosen one, the woman I have been searching for for a long, long time, over a century—the only one who sees me. All others pass by, firmly anchored in their world. But you, ah, you . . . You're different. You hover between realms."

"What must I do?"

"Make love. Become one with me."

"Which world will I belong to?"

"Mine. We'll be lovers for eternity."

The enormity of his words broke through the haze of fascination and lust. "No!" I cried. "This is too much, I can't! I'm not ready!"

His hand let go of my face. I fled and he did not stop me.

I tried to forget. Days were not so bad, but nights were horrible. Feverish with lust and loneliness, my body tossed and turned. It remembered and craved the burning touch of his gentle hands, the caressing sound of a mysterious voice; it pulsated on the brink of temptation. "Feel passion, soar on its wing once, just once. Do it," said the reckless part of me. "No!" screamed sanity. Jordan, Jordan—the name sizzled on my lips.

On the ninth of July, a sultry moonless evening, I gave up. Once, just once, I promised myself.

He was not at the usual place. I paced blindly around the tower, stumbling and scrambling up again. Panic seeped into me, frustrated sobs gurgled in my throat. In sheer desperation, I lurched against a nearby tree to rest my head against its coarse bark.

Suddenly my body tightened in awareness. There was no sound and yet I knew someone was approaching. I did not need to see clearly to know who it was.

Only one man had this effect on my senses.

"Morgan, you know why I am here . . ." he said under his breath.

Silence fell about us. After a while, "Can I return?" was all I could utter.

"Never to me if you go."

"What would happen to you?"

"I can't answer that."

Without a word, he yanked me into his arms, bent his head and kissed me, an urgent, demanding meeting of lips and hot breath. Pressed tightly together, our hands roamed wildly, over and under our garments, discovering each other's contours and leaving a blazing trail wherever they touched. I could feel my life coming out of me, flowing to him, mingling our pulses.

Then, without warning, in the midst of raw desire, Jordan tore himself from the embrace, leaving us both breathless. Holding me at arm length, "Choose. Now," he said.

I swayed forward.

The oldest active light tower on the Great Lakes, Marblehead Lighthouse was built in 1821 and has been a silent witness of history ever since. Its solid stone shore jutting in the lake around the tower gave it its name.

During the Civil War, thousands of Confederate soldiers, mostly officers, were imprisoned on nearby Johnson Island. Cut off from the rest of the world, as they languished on the 300-acre rugged island. We can imagine their lonely gazes peeled to the flashing Marblehead light, the only reminder of human activity within sight.

The keeper's dwelling is now used as a museum.

Michigan City Light, 1875
Indiana

The Catwalk

Battered by a northerly gale, the roof of the lighthouse moaned, walls shuddered; winter wanted to be noticed. Inside, Harriet Colfax rubbed her back wearily. She was tired— no, exhausted. Her head throbbed, her face still burned from the whipping of freezing rain. A pile of damp clothes dried by the wood stove. All night she'd been dashing between the light on shore and the beacon; both had been tricky, demanding constant attention. How often had she rushed into the house to heat the lard to fuel the lanterns? Twice, hampered by wet petticoats, she'd been too slow climbing the tower. Then the blasted sleet had solidified the grease before she'd reached the top, forcing her back.

Not that Harriet was unaccustomed to hard work; she had performed her duties as lighthouse keeper without fail for over twelve years. To the "Great Establishment," as she called it, the light is most important, nothing must interfere with its working. The lights, especially the beacons, steadfast sentinels guiding ships through perils, landmarks to captains, with their insatiable appetite for fuel and shine, had become their keepers' masters.

By midmorning, she had crawled into her narrow bed for a quick nap, but not before dutifully recording the night's events in her log. From the straight spine to the immaculately parted hair, curls severely twisted in a tight bun, everything about Harriet bespoke of duty.

She'd slept fitfully, tossing and turning. She saw dark raging waters snarling, pounding the house, devouring its foundation, tossing her cruelly from one black wave to another, before casting her into the all-consuming belly of the lake. Their wrath seemed prophetic of sinister perils and death. Harriet, normally not fanciful, had awoken with a bitter taste in her mouth and a growing sense of unease. All day she had tried to shake it off, but the rain brought premature darkness, and her normally cozy room became more oppressive as the hours went by.

Duty! Duty! Duty! The wind hammered against the groaning house. Duty had come rolling back in. It was time again to light the beacon. Harriet shivered and walked to the window to assess the weather.

Outside, pounded by a gale unleashing its fury, Lake Michigan shook and snorted. An enormous beast suddenly awakened, stretching its icy paws toward the piers marking the entrance to the harbor, lashing at the solitary beacon, 1,500 feet off the east pier.

In between, rattled and devoured by booming waves crested with white fangs, stood an elevated wooden walkway—the only link between the lighthouse on shore and the beacon. Fifteen hundred feet of swinging wood planks, narrow and slippery, better known as a catwalk, requiring the same agility as its namesake. Harriet's Catwalk.

The beacon, battered and shaken, wailed through the wind-whipped waters. "Come to me Harriet. Light me! For without light I am useless!"

Reliving her nightmare, for the first time in twelve years, Harriet recoiled. "Afraid!" She whispered shrilly, "I am afraid."

The door wrenched open, making her jump. Hair plastered to her face, heavy, sodden skirts dripping under an old oilskin, Ann Hartwell tottered in its opening. The gale roared inside the lighthouse, flinging sleet and icy spray from the lake around her figure, shattering small china, stealing doilies and torturing plants.

"Oh, Harriet, my dear. I had the most terrible dream, didn't have time to tell you this morning before I left for school. Raging waters! Danger! I had to be sure you were all right!" Ann cried over the bellowing squall. The door slammed shut behind her.

The storm, malicious vandal, had brought destruction inside the room, but neither woman paid attention to it. Harriet's grim features greeted her friend of twenty years. No word was needed between the two.

"Oh, my dear, let me make a cup of tea." Ann gasped through water running down her face.

Harriet smiled ironically in spite of herself. "Make me a cup of tea? No. No time. I must light the beacon."

"Must you go?" Ann's voice was barely audible. "The navigation is almost closed, you've had only one entry this week."

Harriet stared. It was unlike Ann to divert her from duty.

"It's the worst storm ever! An uncontrollable fury! The catwalk . . . Harriet, I am afraid." Ann gripped her shoulders.

They locked eyes, both remembering times when waves had dashed over both piers, sweeping over Harriet's head, threatening to sweep her into the lake. Three times ships had rammed into the walkway, breaking large sections of it.

Oh, it would be so easy to stay inside, to give in to the temptation of warmth and safety. No! Harriet shook her head. It was unthinkable. "*The Tawas* has not been through yet. They'll be looking for the light. I'm heating the lard," she said after a while, gently shaking herself free of her friend's grip.

Ann swallowed hard, watching Harriet's every move with the hunger and poignancy of one afraid of seeing a dear friend for the last time.

Harriet kept her eyes on her task. Looking at her petite frame, people expected very little physical strength, but she had shown them!

Nothing in her life had predestined Harriet Colfax, a piano and voice teacher from New York, an educated woman used to soft cushions and pretty dishes, to become a lighthouse keeper, except a twist of fate and an extraordinary will.

Over twenty years before, her only brother had decided to move to Michigan City to start a newspaper. Harriet had quietly said goodbye to the only world she knew and packed her bags. For years she worked as a typesetter in his office, filling her little purse with extra money from piano lessons. Then she'd met Ann Hartwell, a teacher and her soul mate. When her brother decided to move to a warmer climate, she chose to stay, digging her little feet in the soil of their surprised community. Harriet was a woman of surprises, the good people of Michigan City would soon discover to their dismay. They should have noticed the spine, rigid with pride, or the stubborn lift of her chin, the unflinching eyes. Harriet had moved into Ann's small lodgings. Money was tight; the typesetting gone, the piano lessons were not adequate for the needs of a gentle woman. Then she had heard that Mr. Clarkston, the lighthouse keeper, was leaving and that the position would soon be vacant.

"I'm writing to my cousin Schuyler," she had said slyly to Ann one evening. The two were enjoying a quiet moment.

"That's nice," Ann had replied indifferently while leafing through a book.

"Nicer than you think." The laughter in the voice had made Ann raise her head. "Oh?"

"I'm applying for old Mister Clarkston's job."

"Mr. Clarkston . . . the one from the lighthouse?" Ann's puzzled expression made Harriet smile.

"Yes, the very same. He's leaving, I'm applying for the position," she said, coolly folding her letter.

Ann had jumped, shaking her head with incredulity. "What? You don't know anything about—"

"That's right, but I am going to learn. It's $350 a year, plus supplies—a nice income, the answer to my troubles."

"You'll never get the job, not with so many men wanting it," Ann had admonished.

But Harriet knew how to win. "Yes, I shall." She brandished her letter. "Schuyler is a member of Congress, and a good friend of General U.S. Grant," she added mischievously.

In a time when navigation aids came under the aegis of the

Treasury Department, and many lighthouse keepers were po-
litical appointees, Harriet beat the competition.

As bold as brass, ignoring whispers and angry looks, Harriet
and Ann had moved their belongings to the lighthouse, upset-
ting the townsfolk. She's too small, too gentle, the people said;
she's just a piano teacher they wrote. She'd proven them all wrong.

"Is this our place? It's lonely—and wet." Ann had whispered, when first seeing the place. "I don't like water." After all
those years her dreams still turned to the land; she never even
dipped a toe in the lapping water.

But the shrill winds and shimmering waters had brought a
dewy glow to Harriet's cheeks. "It's beautiful," she murmured
every morning when the sun and breeze kissed her new home
with a cold spray.

What had been a solution to penury had become a calling.
How often had Harriet lovingly shone the light on the lake,
polished the lamps, and greeted passing ships? It was a pleasant life, agreeable to her temperament.

Then two years ago, the Lighthouse Board added the beacon
and its catwalk. Harriet's life had changed forever; the two
buildings bore grimly in her inner heart, constant reminders of
the cold reality of her calling.

"It's ready," she said, pouring the melted lard in its container. "Can you pass me my oilskin?"

Ann flinched, her eyes shiny pools.

Harriet returned a glimmer of a smile and hugged her friend
fiercely. "I'll be all right." Forced heartiness lifted her tone.

Ann bravely waved an assenting hand. Harriet could feel
Ann's loving eyes following her to the door.

Outside, the freezing gale, relentless master of the elements,
slapped Harriet about, entwining her skirts around her ankles,
biting into her flesh. She surveyed the stretch of dark water
roaring between the beacon and shore. Teeth clenched, bent
against the wind, struggling to keep her balance, Harriet
reached the catwalk. She groped for the rail with one hand,
clutching the container of lard with the other. She took one
step; the freezing weather had made the wood slippery and she

fell to her knees. The shock made her gasp. Up she went, cursing the rush of snarling foam dashing over the rails, blinding her with spray. She had to reach the lantern room before the lard congealed.

Her small figure hugging the rail, breathless, she staggered forward, one stubborn step at a time, her mind hammering, "The beacon! The beacon! Light the beacon."

Harriet had just reached the beacon ladder when a gigantic wave burst out of the chasm in a last attempt to swallow an intruder in the heart of the storm. It crashed over her, sweeping away her precious container, nearly carrying her into the gaping black mouth of the lake. One icy hand tightly coiled around a rung of the ladder, the other, suddenly empty, hung close to her heaving chest. Spitting and gasping, she dangled and stared through her wet lashes.

The walkway had been swept away.

Water crashed upon her frail body, sucking her in its powerful grip, loosening her fingers. Heart racing, thumping into her ear, grunting, she tightened her grip on the step. Up! Up! She must go! Each crashing breaker gnawed at her strength; each shriek of the wind shook her very soul. Half-drowned, groping blindly for the ladder, lost beyond all thoughts but pure survival, she scaled the beacon. Almost there! In at last!

She staggered inside. I'm alive! she thought. I'm alive. And she slumped against a wall of the lantern room. Immured in the relative safety of her turret, Harriet's thoughts began to assail her in a jumble. *The Tawas* would no longer find its way to the harbor! Ann, who'd watched her disappear into the encroaching waters, might believe her drowned! Ann who was afraid of water and did not swim!

With the dark came an amplification of the noise. The booming of the waves as they punched the beacon roused in her the fear that had lain crouched in her breast since the morning. Brutally assaulted, the tower shook with the furious force of the seething lake. Windows shattered all about, the storm burst upon her. The walls began to shudder rhythmically with each onslaught.

Harriet realized with an ego-shattering shock that she was terrified. She fell on her knees, deafened by the roar, contemplating death in the back-mouthed waves.

The tower groaned. She thought she heard a sickening, rumbling noise. She held her breath. Another groan. Harriet felt a reshuffling of stones, a shudder, the sound of struggle between elements and structure. She quickly crossed herself.

Then, suddenly, as if to atone for its wickedness, or to gather strength, Harriet did not know which, the storm abated slightly. The hissing and clawing of the surf settled down. Forcing her aching body up, spurring it with the terror boiling inside her, Harriet scrambled to her feet to peer over the lake before the storm again engulfed it. Was it a hallucination? A vision? A dark shape seemed to dance over the crested water.

Muffled by the quieted wind, a screech shivered across the lake. Heart hammering, trembling fingers clenched on her chest, Harriet strained to listen. "Harrieeet! . . . Haaaarieeet!"

The tower rumbled once again.

"Help! Help!" she screamed hoarsely, again.

The dark shape came closer. Crying tears of relief—and fear—Harriet identified it immediately. Erratically advancing on the crested waves was the lighthouse rowboat, Ann struggling to keep it afloat. Ann who did not swim. Dear God!

"Go back! You'll drown!" She screamed. Her own death would be accounted to duty but Ann did not need to die. "Go back!"

Ann continued to row.

The beacon tottered.

Harriet quickly scrambled down the ladder. "Here! Here!" She hung from the last step, hoping to lower herself in without tossing them both in the water. She could see Ann valiantly straining to control the small craft.

Harriet waited for a wave to lift the boat higher. In!

"Quickly," she shouted and grabbed the oars, rowing beyond endurance in a bid for safety.

Behind them, the beacon, vanquished by the elements; gave one last shudder before being swallowed by the leaden foam. It could have been me, thought Harriet. It could have been me.

Harriet Colfax retired in 1904 at age 80, after having performed her duties for 43 years. A year later Ann Hartwell died, and Harriet, lonely without her dear friend, followed her a few months later. She had an unblemished record.

The Michigan City lighthouse now is a museum.

Oswego West Pierhead Light, 1942 and 1994
Lake Ontario, Oswego, New York

The Monument

Oswego, 1994

The still surface of Lake Ontario was only broken by the wake of the little cutter taking U.S. Coast Guard Chief Tim Moore and me to the Oswego lighthouse. He and his crew went to install a solar-powered lens in the old tower; and I, Melanie Belcher, a journalist and photographer for the *Toronto Star*, went to take a few pictures.

Now and then the Chief sighed. With relief. The new lens installed, at last the door would be shut tight on one of his outfit's most dreaded assignments.

Yesterday, my boss had tossed a map on my desk. "Hey, Melanie. They're locking up the Oswego light. Have to. It's packed with asbestos. 'Glad to shut the door on it, I expect. Plenty of rumors. Cover it."

Old Greensberg did not need to tell me where Oswego is. Although its site now belongs to the U.S., it is very much part of our Canadian history. The light stands at the mouth of the Oswego River, where it empties into Lake Ontario, near Fort Ontario, the location of many battles during colonial times.

Several rolls of microfilm and a few interviews later, I banged

51

my briefcase shut, scoffing at the results of my investigation, dismissing them as folk tales—no, drivels—convinced that such nonsense would never affect me.

And yet . . .

Men and women—steadfast storm fighters who did not hesitate to ride a bull of a sea, groping and gasping under the blows of leaping waves in order to save lives—winced at the notion of entering the light.

Yes, it was packed with asbestos.

Yes, the wind often hammered against the groaning house and churning waters pounded its foundation.

Yet all of this, menacing enough to less stalwart souls, paled in comparison to the light's reputation.

Haunted.

Tormented by a disturbing past.

Discontented spirits wandering sadly within its walls.

Several regulars talked, always in hushed tones, of strange happenings; of ghostly footsteps echoing in the tower above their heads; of dashing up the rambling stairs, blood beating thickly in their ears, to find no one there but themselves. Doubt and fear mingled in their minds, wrestling with logic.

Some complained, even the most jovial, of a pervading feeling of bitter misery, of being aware of a presence without seeing it. Others murmured, suppressing a shiver, about tightening screws, installing new light bulbs, to find their work undone while turning their backs.

When a billowing darkness engulfed the tower and the strained voices of ship captains came over the radio, a strange, flickering light suddenly appeared at the window, guiding them to safety.

The old ones, seeing it from the shore, quickly crossed themselves, names spilling out of their twisted mouths like prayers on a rosary. "Ira Dell . . . Allen Wagner . . ."

They remember, they said, December 4, 1942.

A few phone calls to the U.S. Coast Guard later, I received permission to accompany Tim Moore on his mission, and mine—my self-appointed task of squelching all gossip, of proving there was nothing to fear at the lighthouse. Here I was, cameras and tripod around me, pen and pad in hand, ready to interview Tim Moore, a touch of arrogance starching my back.

"Close the door on it, I have said it many times," Moore murmured between tight lips while staring hard at the horizon. "Shoot. Go ahead, ask me questions," he said with a hint of steel in his voice, in the manner of a man accustomed to controversy.

First, I needed the facts. Moore was a well-esteemed, no-nonsense man; the openness of his gaze, his firm gait and strong handshake clearly showed that. The lore would come after, probably not from him, he was too solid for such gossip. "In your own words, what happened in 1942?"

Moore's brooding face darkened. "A savage day, a tragic accident, one that left lasting sorrow in the heart of the region." He paused, lost in thoughts.

"Tell me." I said softly. Experience had taught me that gentle coaxing went a long way.

So deep in the past was his mind that it took the Chief a visible effort to refocus on the present. "It was three days before the closing of the shipping traffic for the season.

"As keeper Alan Murray readied to be relieved from duty at the light, a storm of unprecedented fury began to rage over the lake, and Murray was cut off from the shore by winds exceeding sixty miles per hour." He pointed to a rocky structure. "See this breakwall? That's the only link to the mainland, and it was all iced over, too treacherous to attempt a rescue by land. Chief Peterson and several regulars tried to launch a boat, but waves of titanic dimensions forced them back. So, old Murray was forced to batten down in his tower and to resume his duties."

"How long did he stay there?"

"Three days, three long days of churning seas. Remember that in those times the lights required round-the-clock attention, one can easily imagine Murray's exhaustion." Pain passed over his face. "At last, on the third day, the winds abated to thirty miles per hour, the waves looked more manageable, and Peterson was anxious to relieve his keeper. So anxious."

I'd lost him again. "What happened?" I prodded.

"Good God!" he muttered at length. "Clearly forgot about

you!" He shook his head to clear it. "Peterson and eight men set out in a 38-foot boat. They reached the dock without too many problems and began the transfer of Murray to the boat and two fresh tenders to the light. Peterson was backing up when a horrible set of circumstances changed their luck. First his engine died out, leaving him and his men at the mercy of the lake, then out of nowhere, a gigantic wave surged forward, picked up the boat as though it were a toy, overturned it and smashed it against the foundation of the lighthouse."

I gasped and shuddered. "What . . . What about the men?"

Moore's brow was dark with sorrow. "Six men fell in the water, including twenty-one-year-old Allen Wagner, a well-liked youth in the community. Two men were fortunate enough, if such can be said, to be trapped on the boat. They plunged into the icy lake and managed to crawl onto the wall. Poor souls."

His voice had become shaky, and he stopped to control it. I lowered my gaze. "They were exhausted. Helpless, they watched their comrades being engulfed by the waves, even young Wagner who fought the frigid waves so courageously until the cold seized his limbs and he disappeared under water."

In silence I gulped, my mouth filling with bile.

Slowly, Moore continued. His words, simply chosen, vibrated with compassion, admiration and sadness. "Dell and Bay were picked up by another boat, and after barely warming up, joined the search for the bodies of their comrades."

Faced with such sorrow, such heroism, my resolution to dispel gossip was shaken. I let Moore recover for a moment. "What about the rumors, sir? The strange happenings at the light?" I asked in a faint voice, aware of the indecency of my question, yet determined to complete my assignment; Moore, after all, would be reasonable.

"Rumors?" Moore gave an indignant shrug of his shoulder, causing my eyebrows to knit in a perplexed expression. "You mean facts, Ms. Belcher. My people do not fabricate stories, their bravery is common knowledge," he continued stoutly. "Let me tell you a few things, just in case the importance of the report does not sink in (I chose to ignore the insult). Six men died in the line of duty, six men whose names do not

figure on any monuments and whose heroism remains offi-
cially ignored. It's my people and the old folks who keep their
memory alive. Those men are still waiting for their due. That's
why there is trouble at the light."

In spite of myself, a slight mist obscured my vision. I did not
bother to wipe it.

Moore clenched his jaws. "Never bothered to raise a monument . . . not a darn thing!"

"Nothing?" I choked.

"Always an excuse. First it was World War II—we could understand that—but then another pretext, and another. The families were promised a monument. Nothing." The Chief grew somber. "It is said that the light will be troubled until the matter has
been properly settled. Today I shall lock the door, but inside live
the spirits of six men whose unfinished business will continue
to haunt the tower until they are given their due."

I could not suppress a smile. However wrenching the accident had been, I was not easily disposed to change my view on
ghosts and supernatural occurrences.

Fortunately we were docking. Ignoring my amused face,
Moore lifted his gaze to the lantern room. "Where will you
begin shooting first? Just so we keep out of each other's way."

"The tower. I'll be quick."

He thought for a moment, pursing his lips in concentration.
"Bob can go with you . . ."

"Thanks. Not necessary." I thought myself to be a woman
of proven self-sufficiency, beyond the needs of protection.

He opened his mouth with the air of a man with serious
matters to consider, but thought better of it.

I clambered up the stairs to the tower and began setting up
my gear. Outside, the lake looked calm, nothing unusual, only
water and the blue sky. The sun shone hard through the glass
and soon the heat forced me to roll up my sleeves.

After spending some time familiarizing myself with the tower
and selecting a spot for my tripod, I began working. Oddly, until
that moment I had not noticed how silent the room was. The
muffled voices of the men assembling their equipment outside
came through the walls, but inside—inside was different.

Something was happening; there was a peculiarity in the air, the nature of which I did not understand, but I could not put down my thoughts nor fix my mind upon my task. An oppressing chill fell into the room. I did not bother to button down my sleeves, for I knew, really *knew*, that it was the sort that no amount of clothing could dissipate. It belonged to a world beyond mere flesh and blood—it clung to the soul.

Haunted. Tormented by a disturbing past.

I became nervous. Perhaps it was but the silly stories about the light that disturbed me so. I forced myself to resume work, if only to prove to myself that reason prevails. My fingers trembled as I suppressed the impulse to call out for help.

A muffled breathing. A light caress upon my shoulders, as light as wind. Tim Moore! Without shifting my gaze, I cried breathlessly, "Hard climb, Chief, isn't it?"

No answer. I peered over my shoulder, around the lens.

I was alone.

There is nothing to fear. Nothing to fear.

To work required summoning a firmness of will I hardly possessed. A movement, something, hovered on the edge of my consciousness—a spirit, an entity? Such was the state of my demented mind that, against all logic, my brain accepted the idea. I felt weak, trapped and awaiting the mercy of whatever inhabited the tower.

Hair prickling on the back of my neck, for a moment I was sure someone stood behind me. I think I shrieked then. My heart beat thickly in my ears. My eyes caught a dazzling glare coming from the lens. My mind froze, afraid of what it would find there. I looked wildly around the room, panic gradually overcoming me. Mad or sane, it did not matter any more.

There on the lens, again! This time a dark lump, no, the outline of a human being came slowly into view, gradually taking shape before me. I stared hard, then rubbed my eyes and stared harder still.

But as the images developed more distinctly, the sensation of fear I had felt a second ago gave way to something more frightful. I slumped against the wall.

I was surrounded by a billowing blackness, composed of sea

and sky commingled, thundering against me from all sides. On the lens, the figure, a man, was standing on the icy platform of the lighthouse, holding a lantern in trembling hands, its light flickering in the howling elements. I guessed he was the keeper. Ice, ice, everywhere—on the platform, on the breakwall. I felt its grip, I saw it on the keeper's oilskin. He was shouting, waving his arms frantically, but the storm outroared his voice, the waves crashed against the lighthouse in deafening tumult.

A dark shadow approached—a boat, with several men onboard, fighting its way through the wild and raging water. Its approach and the roaring of the storm caused me to tremble.

Suddenly, the lake surged forward in a savage onslaught and tossed the boat in the air, overturning it and smashing it against the foundation of the light. Men were strewn as puppets in the booming chasm. I screamed—a hoarse, half-choked sob. Two men dragged themselves over the ice and onto the wall, clinging onto the blocks of frozen water. The keeper bellowed lustily as he made his way toward them with frenzied effort.

Others disappeared in the abyss. Gone forever. A long stab of grief drove through my heart and I sobbed noisily in misery.

Then, I saw him.

Alone.

He began to swim, and my soul penetrated his heart. I searched his face, his eyes; his distress became mine. He swam mechanically with the practiced strokes of a young man not too long out of school, uttering feverish prayers, the words stumbling into one another from his frozen lips. He fought the waves furiously without getting anywhere.

Hope gave way to despair.

He was alone, abandoned to the fury of the elements. Oh, what a terrible thing it is to be alone!

Sobbing with helplessness and frustration, he beat the water with his arms. Fatigue turned into exhaustion, already the icy lake held his limbs in a deadly grip. Hopelessness, loneliness, an overwhelming sense of an inescapable fate fell upon him. He moaned tragically and stopped swimming.

The fight was over.

A last prayer tumbled out of his deathly-pale mouth, not

the supplicating type, but the words of reconciliation one murmurs an instant before death. The physical demise began to clutch him. Three times, he went down gasping, calling God between each ragged breath, and then, throwing up his arms, he sank in a world of eternal frigidity.

Trembling from head to foot, I closed my eyes.

"Everything all right in here?" A voice made me jump in abject terror; the Chief's concerned face poked through the door. Sweat dripped in great beads down my body. My eyes darted to the lens. It took me long puzzled moments to realize that the lens shone brightly, devoid of tragedy.

I swallowed big gulps of air and light, welcoming the reality of the present. A dream, a vision, an hallucination? I tried to collect my thoughts and pointed with a shaking hand.

The Chief quickly reached to me. "You've seen them, too."

"You mean . . ." I stammered. Full understanding then came to me. "You mean, 1942?"

Although Melanie Belcher and Chief Moore are fictitious, the story, as told in Moore's interview, is true. The names of the men have been changed to protect the feelings of relatives of the deceased. In 1994, the light was automated by Coast Guard Chief Lt. Ed Brown because of its asbestos content. According to an article written by Sean Kirst (*Lighthouse Digest*, January 1997), one of the young men's fathers, David Irving, 98, was still alive in 1996. Fred Ruff, one of the survivors, won't even go near the place. Both are still waiting for a monument. And waiting, and waiting . . .

Three different lighthouses have guided shipping vessels into the busy port of Oswego. The first, a simple stone tower and dwelling, was erected in 1822 at Fort Ontario. As traffic increased on Lake Ontario, a more powerful one was built on the west side of the Oswego harbor. In 1934, the present light was established and the previous one pulled down, to the dismay of several generations of keepers and their descendants.

The Oswego lighthouse is not opened to the public but can be seen from Oswego, where its distinctive flashing red light has become a landmark to many sailors.

Grand Traverse Light, 1852
Lake Michigan

Need Help?

It was a beautiful morning. Tiny waves nibbled and spat at the rocky shoreline of Cat Head Point on Lake Michigan with unrelenting energy, the way children do on the first day of vacation. His chest raised proudly, Ross McLeod cast a satisfied eye around him.

Among a clump of large trees, a construction crew was building his lighthouse. It was almost finished and its two story building and square tower already dominated Grand Traverse Bay, marking the entrance. In another two weeks Ross could move in.

Although Congress had voted for its establishment and was paying for it, Grand Traverse lighthouse belonged to Ross, spiritually if not technically, as much as he belonged to it. Privately, Ross called it his.

He had been chosen as its first keeper, the first to climb its stairs to the lantern room and breathe the scent of fresh paint. Most important, he would be the first to shine its glorious

Fresnel lens, especially imported from France and painstakingly assembled the day before.

Other keepers would come later, but they would only emulate him. He had watched the construction of his lighthouse with the anxiety of a new father; like one, he would defend it with his life.

After one last look over his domain, Ross checked the list of supplies the foreman had prepared. It was long, as usual. They were several miles from town and did not go to the stores very often. He reloaded his Smith & Wesson—these were unsecured times, one had to be prepared, and Ross certainly was. "I'm taking the skiff!" he yelled over his shoulder to no one in particular. The foreman mopped his forehead and waved an assenting hand.

A warm breeze blew lazily across the lake. After hoisting the main and setting on a tack, Ross idly leaned back against the transom. His gaze wandered across the varicolored water without seeing anything, except the dreams that drifted through his sun-soaked head. His reverie swept onward to impending glory. He would be a model of virtue, executing every rule rigidly described by the Establishment; he would tend the lighthouse well, according to the book. It would become a real showplace.

He could see himself on Sundays, showing people the beautiful hand-polished prisms of his Fresnel lens. "'Shipped across the Atlantic in pieces and assembled here. 'Can throw light fourteen miles or more on the horizon," he'd say, pausing in his speech to let that impressive piece of news sink in. "Just think. We have a Fresnel, the latest in technology." Up and down he would go for most of the day, awestruck visitors in tow. They would come from long ways away, maybe even as far as Detroit.

The Great Plan implementation had begun yesterday with the assembly of the lens.

Close to Northport a few clouds gathered in the blue sky. The screeching of the seagulls, which earlier had filled him with happiness, now echoed with unexplainable foreboding. He shivered.

In town, instead of dawdling as usual, exchanging pleasantries with the locals and stopping at the shanty to see Bill and get an earful of gossip for the boys, Ross hurriedly purchased his goods and stowed them securely in the hold of his skiff. A peculiar and disturbing feeling of urgency had entered his mind and would not leave it. Something unexplainable was compelling Ross, a sturdy man of no fanciful imagination, back to the light.

Better cast off. One hand untying a line, Ross shook his head. What's the matter? A few screeches and dark clouds and you want to leave? A vision of the crestfallen faces of the building crew, "What, no news?" made him stop. Willfully, he pushed all thoughts of impending disaster from his mind and secured the line again.

Inside the shanty, he leaned against the bar and waited, glancing about. Two men were loitering at the counter and three others played a game of poker at one end of the room. Ida Hawkins, the proprietor's wife, idly watched the play, slugging whiskey and puffing on a cheroot, her black hat pulled down low over her eyes. The butt of a Colt .45 shone brightly against her chest. Always ready to fire, Ida wore her six shooter in a shoulder strap. She kept a clean table, honest game and stiff drinks. Cheaters and gunslingers—the lucky ones—lay low; others lay six feet under.

Bill, her husband, a peaceful, scrawny fellow, had blissfully thrown his gun at the bottom of a drawer on their wedding night and had never touched it since. Day after day he enjoyed doing what he liked best—cooking and gossiping—under the undisputed protection of his wife. The pair was quite devoted to each other.

Ida ambled over. Ross tensed imperceptibly. Careful, a niggling voice said to his brain. She was a big, strapping woman, unpredictable and yet friendly with a few. Hat on, she had a couple of inches on him. Ross sucked in his belly and straightened his spine.

"How's it going?" she said, slapping him across the shoulders with a whack that almost sent him reeling. He rubbed his neck and stepped back, wondering why he had bothered coming in—another of Ida's amiable gestures might send him flying across the room.

"Coming along," he sputtered through tight lips.

She slid behind the counter. "The usual?"

Ross nodded with a forced smile. "Bill here?"

"'O'Haras'. Potatoes." Ida was faster with her gun than with her words. Guessing that Bill had gone to buy a potato supply at the O'Haras', Ross squelched his disappointment. There wouldn't be much gossip to report.

Ida leaned forward, her eyes boring into his. "Bothered at the Cat?"

"No."

"Let me know," she said, grinning broadly. Nothing brought Ida more pleasure than a good gun scrape. There had been plenty of that lately. James Strang had moved his Mormon community to nearby Beaver Island and proclaimed himself king of that land two years before. Since then, bloody battles regularly exploded between the local Irish potato farmers and some of Strang's disciples. Now the same violence and lawlessness were spreading to the mainland.

"Thank you," he replied acidly. "And here?"

She patted her Colt and smiled complacently. "There's been plenty. All gone."

Ross found himself becoming very irritated. She had no right to smile like that, to feel so clever, to even suggest he might need help—her help. Ida Hawkins, he thought gloomily. Big troubles. I do not want an Ida Hawkins meddling in my affairs. Then, he laughed at her arrogance, and his, and was about to toss his drink when he stopped. The door behind him crashed open. In strode a heavy-booted man. "Bandits!" he shouted. "A whole gang of them, sailing straight for the Cat, screaming and shouting!"

All was silent for a moment.

"You don't suppose they would . . ." began Ross in alarm.

Ida shot from behind the bar and shoved him rudely out of her way. "Shut up, McLeod!" she barked, clutching her Colt. "Follow me!"

Ross stiffened in resentment, but suddenly remembering his light, his lens and his dreams, he flew in such a rage that all other emotions disappeared. He stormed outside in Ida's wake, heart burning with white searing fury. The men from the shanty followed close behind.

Ida jumped into his skiff. Mercifully the wind had picked up speed; the craft plunged across foamy crests, the breeze hissing in its main. Ross pulled the sails in tightly, flirting dangerously with the breeze and spray.

Near Cat Head, he loosened the sheets and raised a warning hand to the other crafts.

Above the noise of the flapping sails, a gun shot echoed sharply. A flock of seagulls squawked and flew chaotically over the area, shielding the light. His heart jumped, and he felt a little sick, but anger, as hot as melting copper, soon clenched his fists and tightened his jaw. As bold as the blue sky, those bandits were attacking his lighthouse! A roar formed on his lips, but Ida swiftly smothered it with her hand. "Quiet, McLeod!" she hissed in his ear.

Swallowing his yells of fury, Ross tightened the sheets and tacked toward the shore, signaling to the others. They beached behind the wooden area, a little way from the clearing. Ida jumped out and silently ordered everyone to follow her with a wave of her pistol. Guns in hand they dropped to the ground, and, as swift and silent as slithering snakes, crept through the woods.

From behind an oak, Ross saw an incredible scene of rampage. Protected by the remoteness of the place, men, he could see five, were ransacking his home; they hauled his newly-installed stove and his trunks the length of the yard toward the water. The construction crew, eight men, was laying face down on the ground, two bandits holding guns over their heads. Next to them, the figure of a worker clutching his middle tumbled out, staggered a few paces, and fell at the feet of a heavy-booted renegade. Sweat drizzling down his back, chest hurting, Ross' brain went temporarily dead.

But when a man shouted, "Boys, let's get the lens!" an overpowering rage overtook him. Fiendish brigands! Without thinking, Ross put on an incredible spurt of speed and flew across the woods. Clucking her tongue in disgust, Ida stopped others with an imperious hand.

Before he had time to reach the clearing, a swift blow to the head sent Ross crashing to the ground. When he came to, he was laying flat on his back, his hands tied tightly together in front of him with strong cord. An outlaw, his head covered with a dirty brown hat and his face hidden by a dusty handkerchief, took two menacing steps forward. He clutched his gun in readiness. The glint in his bloodshot eyes was clearly evil. "Get up! Do as I say! I—"

The point of a Colt ramming sharply into his back put an abrupt end to his threats.

"Not so fast, mister!" hissed Ida. "Drop the gun!"

A wicked smile spread on the bandit's face. "Look, here, lady . . ."

Unfortunate choice of word. Ida did not care to be a lady. One more savage shove. "Hey, ain't no call for that!" he gasped through rotten teeth.

In a motion so swift that nobody could tell what she'd done, Ida had knocked the gun off the gangster's hand and spun him around. "I said, drop it," she spat in his face. His broken wrist dangled at an odd angle.

"Gus, untie McLeod. All yours," she said, showing her prisoner to Ross shaking the rope loose. Ida pulled her hat down lower over her eyes, not quickly enough to hide a definite gleam of excitement. "Okay, boys, let's get them."

A few minutes later, cheers and applause broke into the clearing. Ida and her posse stood in the middle of seven tightly bound men.

Ross sighed with relief.

"Hey! McLeod! Call me next time you need me!" She shouted.

"I will," he grinned. And he meant it.

The Grand Traverse Lighthouse is located in the Leelanau State Park at the end of the narrow peninsula that stretches northward into Lake Michigan and marks the entrance to the Grand Traverse Bay.

Its first keeper was Philo Beers, a U.S. Deputy Marshal. Legend claims that while the light was under construction James Strang and a band of outlaws attempted to raid it and dismantle the Fresnel lens. Bad move! Philo Beers was on duty.

The light is no longer in service, but the large two-story building is now a museum filled with antiques and mementos.

Saint Martin Island Light, 1900 and 1910
Green Bay

Edward

1900, in a house somewhere on the shore of one of the Great Lakes.

Edward watched Harley from the corner of one eye. Harley, the nasty little creep who gutted his victims like fish after sex, was in a good mood. Edward knew why. The ringing of the doorbell confirmed his suspicions. An obese woman entered, mountainous breasts jiggling around a fake, partly molted fur boa that reeked of naphthalene.

Harley liked them poor and overweight; he found mounds of soft jellylike flesh wildly exciting. This time his craving was strong, Edward could tell. The rapid breath, wetting of lips, noisy scratches between the legs; all were a bad omen for the woman–Harley's response to sexual arousal involved pain–unfortunate for his victim, but vastly satisfying for Edward.

He always got the head.

Well, not always. Of late, Harley, the nasty cretin, had gotten meaner. Dangled one in front of him the other day, just as he needed sustenance very badly. Then threw it in the wood stove, the blackguard did, and left Edward shaking with hunger. And perplexed and disoriented. Whilst any odd limb could satisfy his belly, only brains sustained his cunning.

Edward settled back and waited, as still and quiet as he could be. He stared at the contortions of the naked bodies, waiting and waiting, hope pulsating through his massive body. He was ravenous. A surge of panic washed over him—what if Harley kept all the joy to himself?

When Harley raised the knife Edward almost lost control. He couldn't help it. The smell of fear, an arousing mixture of sweetness and tartness, always did that to him. His gills fluttered and his mouth opened, showing rows of razor-sharp teeth.

The woman on the bed heard the sound behind her and caught a movement in the gigantic tank. She turned, eyes bulging with terror, both transfixed and appalled, "What . . ." she began to scream as Harley struck her in the belly.

Edward kept still through the screams, the hacking and ripping. When a groan finally told him Harley had climaxed, he splashed the water to remind him of his presence. The man lifted his hand from the dead breast he was carving to toss Edward a foot, a leg and a rib; anything but what he knew Edward really craved.

"Here, take that! And that!" Harley was laughing. Laughing! A demonic high-pitched screech—the sort emitted by sadistic cowards who, after years of being bullied, at last release their pent-up anger on a weaker one. Edward in the sea was powerful, his jaws and dorsal fin ruled the waters, but Edward in a tank was helpless, an exquisite situation as far Harley was concerned.

Edward squirmed frantically. No, the head! The head!

Harley scrambled up and seized the head, snickering. "Here, pretty, pretty. Is this what my baby wants?"

Edward reared up in a frenzy, mouth gaping. Blood dripped on his snout. He gulped it wildly. More! More! More!

Harley, the bully, dipped and retracted the head; tantalizing, tormenting, close enough for the shark to smell its sweet aroma, but never within his reach. Tail thrusting, Edward strained to grab it. His frenzied contortions brought fits of laughter to Harley's puny chest.

Enough! Edward's next move wiped the smirk off the man's face. Stupefied, he saw the shark give a vigorous thrust. In one swift motion, the powerful jaws snapped around the head and the hand holding it. Got it!

"Damn it!" Harley screamed through ragged breath, and stumbled to the floor. Cradling against his chest bloody strands of sinew where his right hand used to be, he groped for the knife.

He lurched toward the tank, left hand raised to strike.

Sensing danger, Edward lunged mightily, desperately. He rammed his powerful snout into the man's chest with such force it knocked him backward to the floor. As though drunken, Harley scrambled up, still holding his weapon. Trembling with the effort, saliva bubbling at the mouth, he clutched the knife above his head, then, swaying, lost his balance. His body tumbled closer, oh, ever so close. Too close.

Man and fish gazed at each other. A nameless terror constricted Harley's chest.

Fear again. Edward smelt it, relished it. In a single heaving motion, he rose from the tank, snapped his gaping mouth around his tormentor's neck and torso and bit hard. But his thrust had been too high, too strong. It pitched them both to the ground.

For a split second, Harley felt a searing pain, a squeeze followed by a rush of viscous warmth in his throat. "I'm being eaten," was his last thought before he died.

At first, Edward was too starved, too busy gorging himself to suffer from his alien surroundings. He bit and tore and gulped, leaving the head for last, vaguely thinking that it did not taste as good as the women's. It would not go down, so he spat it out.

Harley was most indigestible.

Only then did he notice his searing breath, the burning ache in his gills and membranes, and the drying and wrinkling of his usually sleek skin. Instantly alert, he became aware of his hostile environment. He must seek water, now, soon, or he would not survive.

1910, Saint Martin Island Light

It was a gray, windless morning. Fog was in the air. The duskiness of night still clung to low-hanging clouds, and would probably hang over the lake until the evening, when complete darkness cloaked the island in inky shades.

Lenore shivered and chewed on her bottom lip as she packed her sons' lunch basket; leftover chicken for seven-year-old Tim, hard-boiled eggs and a little salt wrapped in paper for twelve-year-old Eric. He was very fond of salt.

Lenore did not like the lake, never took to it, and she liked even less having her children row over to Washington Island to attend school. Every morning, she stood by the lighthouse's little dock and, nervously swallowing, stared at their retreating backs.

"'Taking your lunch to the boat," she said over her shoulder. Ever since the day the boys had forgotten their basket and had to spend the whole day without food, Lenore had placed it inside their rowing boat herself.

Outside, Jack was smoking a pipe, calmly watching a freighter nose its way to Lake Michigan. She stood by her husband, staring fixedly at the vast stretch of leaden water where puffs of fog had began to curl, "A terrible force," she muttered, "a terrible force."

The freighter bellowed and plowed by at top speed. It rushed as though chased by the devil, warning others of unseen perils, of an upcoming tragedy.

At the sudden noise, the unusual speed, something snapped inside Lenore. She turned pale and shuddered violently. A wild and terrible fear clutched her throat—nothing like her habitual nervousness—no, this time she was sick with apprehension.

Today, more than ever, she did not want her children on the lake.

Jack was a good man but he could be difficult, quite intractable in fact, and never had much patience for his wife's fearful notions. A hardened mariner, years of duty as keeper of the light on a small island had not improved his inflexibility. With a fake nonchalance that would not have duped a child, Lenore emitted a thin plea, "I don't think the boys should go to school today."

"Nonsense, my dear. Stop mollycoddling them, they'll be perfectly all right," he stated between two puffs on his pipe with a tone of voice that discouraged any retort.

She returned inside the house, trying to subdue the banging of her heart. The boys were finishing their porridge; Eric, as usual, with his head stuck inside a big encyclopedia. Lenore hovered over them. She managed to appear calm until their departure, but when they prepared to cast off, she cried, "God be with you my children!" and rushed to enfold each boy in a fierce embrace.

She watched them inch their way across the lake. Standing quite still, stiff with the late October morning cold, she listened to the soft splashing of oars, staring fixedly at their retreating backs until she could not see a thing.

The swirling fog had wrapped itself around the fragile little vessel.

She stood there for what seemed an eternity, praying in a cracked voice, clutching her shawl as the minutes ticked by. Feeling an icy rivulet of perspiration trickle down her back, she cursed herself for not arguing with Jack, for allowing her boys to drift into the mounting grayness. She imagined them gliding forever on the glassy surface, saw their terror, and heard their thin voices cry for help, "Mommy, help us! Mommy where are you?"

Like a blind woman she paced up and down the island. She didn't even attend to her hen-house—her proud way of supplementing the family's diet—no, she walked and walked, by turns hysterical and silent.

By midday the fog had thickened to terrible gray, a nightmare. Freighters brayed blindly, calling for Jack's foghorn. When her husband brought her a hot mug of coffee, she was so shaky, she had to wrap both hands around it.

"Come inside," Jack said, prodding her forward.

"No! My sons . . . I want to wait for my sons," she wailed through blanched lips. Despondent, Jack returned to his duty.

The fog and water had been still for hours. It was like moving through a giant wad of cotton wool with no beginning and no end, thought Eric, sitting at the oars. He'd been rowing for so long, so aimlessly, there wasn't a single part of him that did not ache. How long ago had they waved goodbye to their teacher?

Tim balefully rummaged through their empty lunch basket, just a bit of leftover salt and a few crumbs.

Fog stung their lungs and beaded their hair and clothes with dewy drops. In a rush of despair and exhaustion, Eric closed his eyes and sunk his head to his chest.

"Are we . . . are we lost?" Tim cried out fearfully.

Eric peered nervously into the thick grayness. With a forced calmness way beyond his years, he said, "Just taking a rest. We'll be all right. Just hang on."

"I'm cold, so cold, so dreadfully hungry too." Tim was shivering.

Sighing, Eric removed his woolen jacket, tucked it around his younger brother and returned to the oars. Tim's eyes grew moist and enormous, his trembling lips bravely swallowed sobs.

Sadness welled up in Eric at the sight of his brother's scared face. Keep him talking, distracted, he decided. "Hey, the *Henrietta* is coming by with supplies tomorrow," he said lamely. "Mom said the first can of milk will be for rice pudding."

"She did?" A greedy little smile brightened Tim's pinched features.

The even splash of oars pulling against the still water resumed.

But there was fear in the air.

At the bottom of the lake, Edward sluggishly moved through the murky waters. He was exhausted, weak with hunger and confused. For years he had preyed on other fish, innumerable bits of debris and small animals, never replete, never anything human, nothing to nourish his cunning. He must feed soon, human food, or he will die—at least his mental capability will. That he had adapted to fresh water was a biological and evolutionary marvel maintained only by sheer willpower, mind over matter. That was almost gone now, the confusion in his head told him so. His gray body, flat snout, gills and membranes still craved salt. He knew it would always be so.

But food! Food! He needed sustenance, and quickly.

A wave of panic crashed over him. What if nothing came his way? He must seek it then, rise from the depths, go to the light. He must hunt.

Wild with anxiety and hunger, Edward swam a hundred feet toward the surface, hovering a few feet below. Despite increasing exhaustion, he circled larger and larger circumferences, slower, and slower still, till the membranes in his head froze in delight; they picked up a familiar sound, one unheard for years—human voices, only thinner, higher-pitched than usual.

Instantly alert, he raised his conical head to the surface. Something brown, floating in the water ahead, caught his eye.

Then he smelled it—that inimitable, arousing mixture or sweetness and tartness. Fear. Real food, human food, was nearby. He would survive.

He would eat it. Mouth gaping, in a powerful thrust, Edward homed in.

On the island, racked by anxiety, Jack scrambled between the light tower and the foghorn building. Outside, Lenore's prostrate shape made his heart ache with apprehension.

"My sons," he begged, "see the light, hear the horn. Please come home!"

How heavily duty fell on his shoulders! His sons needed help, but helpless, bound by his contract to the Great Establishment to guide ships to safety, the keeper was chained to the light; he could only pray for his sons' protection.

The boys talked in monotonous voices. Tim had taken the oars to give Eric a break. The older boy was wiping the sweat and condensation off his face with his scarf when he heard a powerful splash, more like a savage whipping of the water, behind him. Startled, he swiveled and stared. An unusually large ring of ripples, too big for any fish he knew, was spreading.

"What was that?" Tim shrieked.

"Look over there!" His pulse quickening, Eric pointed at a

tear in the fog. Something gray was bulging out of the water, then disappeared.

Baffled, the brothers exchanged a perplexed glance.

Suddenly, something crashed into the bottom of the boat. It shuddered and heaved violently. Arms flailing, tottering dangerously, the boys managed to land back on their seats.

"Something's under the boat!" screamed Tim.

Another hit. And another. The boat swayed dangerously.

Eric blanched. "We're being attacked!"

They knew not their assailant, nor its reasons, but despite their tender years, recognized approaching death. Blood throbbed in Eric's ears. Quick, do something! Think!

"Quick, give me an oar! Give me an oar!" he yelled.

He will not die waiting, but fighting.

Clutching the oar resolutely, Eric slapped and struck the water blindly, savagely, to try to frighten whatever was attacking them.

Abruptly, the charges ceased. Calm returned to the surface of the lake.

Tim collapsed on his seat. Lips pinched in a thin line, Eric gripped the oar tighter, steeling himself for another assault.

A foghorn, *their* foghorn, brayed into the fog. To die so close to home! Eric wanted to call out. Panic closed his throat.

He noticed a movement and saw the gray mass, the shiny white teeth in the gaping mouth, emerge from the lake. In the conical head, eyes shone with a strange human exaltation. Fifty feet away was a gray dorsal fin. It zigzagged through the water.

Then it came straight at them.

When the time came for the children's return, between two blasts of his foghorn, Jack rushed to Lenore's side, a comforting arm wrapped around her rigid shoulders. Minutes went by. His tense features told her of his growing apprehension. They clung to each other, bereft of words. One hour went agonizingly by, broken only by the keeper's mad dashes to his duty.

Jack's pipe had gone out. She covered her face with trembling hands and began to wail, "My sons, my sons," and collapsed to the ground.

Pale with grief, Jack carried her to bed. The poor woman sank down on the pillow, racked by dry, painful sobs, and stared unseeingly at him, praying incoherently, scarcely knowing where she was. He piled blankets on her frozen body. She clutched his shoulders wildly. "My sons . . . My sons . . ."

He wrenched himself free, crying hoarsely. "I must return to the horn and the light, that's the only thing I can . . ."

The door burst open.

"Mummy! Daddy!" Eric and Tim rushed into the room, breathless.

Lenore wailed piercingly, certain she was gripped by delirium. Jack stood frozen in place. In his sorrow, was he victim to a vision?

The boys threw themselves into the arms of their unbelieving parents who frenziedly clasped and hugged their cold bodies in rapturous embraces, and covered their faces with wild kisses. At last, amid tears of joy and relief, the family let happiness erase horror and grief.

After a while, the parents demanded an explanation.

"We were attacked by a shark!" Eric said breathlessly.

"A shark?" Jack shook his head and looked incredulously at his oldest son. "Impossible," he said after a while.

"It's true! It's true!" shrieked Tim, trembling from head to foot at the memory.

All at once, the boys launched into the telling, each trying to outdo the other.

The father raised a commanding hand. "Stop! Eric, please continue." Eric recounted their being lost on the lake and the ensuing attack.

"He came straight at us!" Tim interrupted, unable to contain his impatience any longer.

"But how did you . . .?" cried Lenore.

"The salt, mother! The salt! My encyclopedia says that sharks live in salt water! We threw it in the lake and he went for it!"

"And we heard the foghorn and rowed over!" added Tim.

At the bottom of the lake, Edward ranted and raved. All lost for a bit of salt! Could not resist it, could you?

You must eat or you will die.

He rose to the surface and began hunting again.

Built in 1905 on St. Martin Island in Green Bay, the six-sided tower is the only one of this type on the Great Lakes.

Children of the successive keepers had to row over to Washington Island to attend school. One day, the children of a keeper got lost in the fog. Their father went searching for them in the night, but they had disappeared without a trace. Since that day, a strange green light is visible wandering along the shore of the island. It is said that the ghost of the father is still roaming about, searching for his long lost children.

Manitou Island Light, 1925
Lake Superior

Dead Calm Sea

Shirley waddled up the stairs and paused in the tower doorway, watching her husband, smiling at his tuneless humming. Bright sunshine illuminated the lantern room. Outside, the gentle roll of the swell bespoke of calm weather. It was a perfect day—as she predicted.

"Hey, Phil?" she said. He was kneeling on the floor, tools and bits of cloth strewn about him, beads of sweat clinging lazily to his brows. The lens had given him trouble all night. "Guess what?"

"What?"

"My labor's started."

His face whitened as if she'd struck it with a fistful of flour. "Shirley. Oh, my God. Are you sure? I mean, it's too early. It's only July second."

She grinned impishly. "I said July, didn't I? July it is."

Shirley had had a low backache all night and had attributed it to the brisk scouring she had done in the kitchen the day before. It was their first child, and she had not guessed that by morn-

77

ing the ache would have turned into a contraction. It left her
catching her breath for the better part of a minute. Phil had
been up all night, tending the light, and she had not wanted to
worry him. By now, distinctive contractions were coming half
an hour apart. A new one hit her hard enough to send her
arching awkwardly against the door frame.

Phil sprang as if propelled by a cannon across the room to
slide a shaking arm around her throbbing body.

"It's all right, Phil." The pain eased and she slowly sank
back against his shoulder.

"Shirley, the skiff—the doctor—the mainland. We must get
you there." How to accomplish this with a dead calm sea, he had
no idea.

She lifted a sweet, reassuring smile. "Don't worry so. Neptune . . ." The pain ate her words.

When the commander had assigned Phil as keeper of the
Manitou light, he had gazed at the young couple pensively, a
faint smile tugging at his mustache. "This report," he had said,
pointing to the file on his desk, "says that you were married only
last month and that you volunteered for the post in the north.
You think it would be pleasant to be alone, that it would be a sort
of . . . an extended honeymoon."

Shirley had flushed crimson and briefly turned shy eyes to
her husband before dipping them to her shoes. Patting her hand,
Phil had smiled charmingly.

The commander had coughed, a deep furrow creasing his
brow and his manner had grown somber. "You understand that
it is an isolated place, half a day's sailing from the mainland."
The young couple nodded, so he continued, "Mr. Knobs is the
keeper, and after he has instructed you in your duties he will go
off and leave you to it."

The lighthouse was a fine old place and Mr. Knobs' rugged
face had broken into a grin at the sight of the pair staring beatifi-
cally at their new station for the first time. The lilac bush was in
full bloom, and a myriad of wild flowers poked their heads through
the rocky soil. Mr. Knobs explained that the approaching sum-

mer brings longer days of sunshine to warm the rocks that hold the heat at nighttime. Soon, due to this condition, everything would bloom and ripen all at once—wild raspberries, blueberries, even goldenrod—a fall flower.

A week later, keeper Knobs had waved them goodbye, and although Phil and Shirley were sorry to see him go, they dismissed him with a pleasant nod.

They were anxious to be alone.

Both had developed a passion for their island and its light equaled only by the intensity of their feelings for each other.

The happy couple often stood on the railing about the lantern, looking across orange lichen-covered rocks, gazing at the shimmering water, at ease with its immensity and changing moods. "Neptune, son of Saturn," Shirley had renamed the Great Superior with the familiarity of untried youth.

When Neptune threw a temper-tantrum, rumbling like thunder, with its acolyte, the wind, riding high on its swollen crests, Shirley and Phil grinned indulgently. Fog was a cocoon for their love; sunshine a painter sprinkling emerald dust on the water and in their hearts. Others feared the unpredictable sea, but they loved Neptune unconditionally. They cleaned and polished and kept vigil over the lake with unflagging enthusiasm.

To many sailors, the light and its keepers, a beacon of safety, had become a tower of joy, of comfort; the foghorn a tallyho of hope. Phil and Shirley's good humor touched everyone. A dish of baked beans always stewed on the purring wood stove and a warm blanket awaited wet shoulders.

"Beware! Beware!" The mariners said, clucking their tongues.

The pair gaily brushed off their warning. "Beware of what? Neptune? He's a friend."

Then Shirley had announced her condition with a peaceful smile. For the first time, apprehension clawed at Phil's heart, but she was so unafraid, so at ease with her changing body that his fears diminished.

"Go now," the captains said to the blushing woman. "We'll take you to the mainland."

She shook her brown curls. "What? And leave Phil?"
So she had stayed longer and longer, and too long . . .

Phil guided her down the stairs, his brow furrowed. He settled her on the bed and raced to the skiff, chiding himself for not getting her to the mainland days ago. He cursed his ignorance about birthing and how babies sometimes come early, without warning. Blast that calm weather! Not a single puff of air to fill his sail!

Less than ten minutes later he panted to a halt at the bedroom door, somewhat bewildered. "The wind! The wind! It's picking up! Just now as I was raising the sail! We'll make it, Shirley! We'll get you there nice and safe!"

Shirley slowly eased herself off the bed and smiled knowingly, "It's Neptune, Phil. I could have told you that."

After Shirley had clumsily climbed into the skiff, Phil hoisted the sail and turned their little gaff-rigged craft into brisk airs.

"Come on, Neptune," Shirley urged. "Give us a push."

As the skiff headed into deeper waters, the bow waves rumbled, and, laying on the bench in the cockpit, she could hear them rushing against the hull. She and Phil had read books about conception and child bearing. Ship captains were only too happy to oblige this charming couple, picking up goods or whatever they required—but their instruction had been as enlightening as ". . . Nature has provided men and women with wonderfully constructed organs for this purpose . . . The mother-to-be must keep herself well and happy . . ." They'd both burst into laughter and closed the books.

The skiff plugged into the wind, Phil constantly adjusting the tiller to keep the sailing balance, Shirley bracing herself against being thrown out of the makeshift bunk. More contractions came and each left her a little more wilted, more gasping for breath. They were going at a great pace and Phil was a bundle of nerves. His tense face and clenched teeth told her of his valiant effort to remain calm and strong. Her love grew deeper for it. She peered, aching, into his eyes and said, "I'm so glad you're here, Phil."

"So am I," he lied. He'd rather be on the mainland with a doctor attending. He pulled in the main.

Then they knew they were too late. A searing pain lifted her midsection off the bunk. "It's time, P-P-Phil," she panted.

"Whaaat?" he cried.

"The baby . . . it's coming!"

"Oh, my God!" He ran a helpless hand through his hair. "Quick . . ."

There seemed to be fifty things to do: Pointing the skiff into the wind, letting go of the sheet, the tiller, slacking away the halyard, lowering the boom and the top par—one eye on his task, the other watching Shirley swallow peaking contractions, futilely gripping her belly to slow the birthing process. "P-P-Phil!"

The sail bellied out, flapping madly from side to side. The noise was terrific. Shirley's eyes filled with terror. "Don't panic! Don't scream!" she told herself. Her fear was etched in the hollow of her cheeks, the beads of sweat on her brow.

Phil belatedly realized that the incredible din was the main cause of her alarm. He grabbed the sail to lash it to the boom; a sudden gust of wind snatched it out of his grip. To his horror, it dropped into the lake, instantaneously filling with water, causing the boat to list dangerously. Shirley grunted and grabbed the shrouds, saving herself from a fall. Grasping the wet sail with both hands, Phil managed to lash it in place. He dropped to Shirley's side.

Another pain contorted her body and Phil had no time to dwell on his next move. He cupped his hands to receive his child. Slimy, purple and wet, their son came and Phil was remarkably calm when he severed the cord linking mother and child with his knife. "Now, breathe, my son," he whispered reverently, "begin your life on earth."

Yes, the baby was born. And still.

Aghast, petrified, Phil looked at his son's bloody face, all bruised and swollen by the birthing ordeal, and so inert. Breathe! Breathe!

Shirley lifted her head. "Is . . . he all right?" She managed through ragged breath.

Phil did not reply, swallowing tears; his mind raced. Come on, breathe! Oh, God! Five seconds went by. Ten. What to do?

Breathe! Breathe! He gave the baby a frightened shake, and another followed by a jerky slap on the wrinkled bottom. Twenty seconds sped by, twenty-five, then thirty. Not a movement, not one sigh from the baby's silent mouth. He heard Shirley whimper, saw his son shrivel within his hands. No! Despair, panic, clawed at him. Another shake.

"Nep-Neptune," Shirley cried through cracked lips. Her words scarcely registered. "Neptune! Save him!" She screamed. "PHIL, GET HIM WET!"

Jolted into action, Phil lay, no, tossed, the baby down on his mother's heaving chest. Scrambling through the hold, he retrieved a bucket, scooped up some water and, in a panic, flung about a gallon of frigid liquid on his wife and baby.

A second later, both hiccuped and the baby started flailing with his arms; he began to bawl lustily, a healthy, wonderful sort of cry. Both parents laughed and sobbed. With joy. With relief.

Hair plastered to her forehead, Shirley shivered. "He's breathing. Th-thanks, Nep-Neptune."

"Saved by the lake!" Phil exclaimed, dropping to his knees.

Shirley nodded soberly. "More water, please, Phil."

Phil looked dumbly at her.

"More water, please," she said with forced patience.

Phil knew better than argue with her. He refilled the bucket, a puzzled frown on his brow.

For a second, Shirley's eyes feasted on the water sloshing in its container. With love, with reverence, she scooped a handful of the liquid and trickled it over her son, herself, over Phil's bent head. "Never be afraid of the lake, my son, it gave you life."

Lifting his gaze, Phil suddenly grew sober. "Shirley, look. No wind." Waves, soft as silk, rustled against the hull.

"I know. Neptune's lullaby."

So the cheerful pair huddled contentedly in the cockpit, their son tucked between them.

Later, after they'd been picked up by a ship, checked by a doctor and declared fit, the young family returned to the Manitou light. Phil wrote in his log: *Lake Superior. One mile*

*west of Manitou light, on July 2, Mrs. Liggett safely delivered
a baby boy. Dead calm sea.*

Manitou Island, surrounded by a ring a gray rocks, lies about
two and a half miles east of the Keweenaw Peninsula. The
island's first lighthouse, a very isolated place, was erected in
1850, but the one standing today—an iron skeletal tower—
dates from 1861 and is one of the oldest structures of this type
on the Great Lakes.

On July 5, 1885, Keeper James Corgan, in a restrained writing fashion typical of official reports, coolly recorded in a log-
book an usual event. Its trauma is humorously belied by his
choice of words: ". . . East of Horseshoe Harbor, Mrs. Corgan
give birth to a rollicking boy; all things lovely, had everything
comfortable aboard. Sea dead calm."

What author could resist such temptation?

Old Presque Isle Light, 1850
Lake Huron, Michigan

Bluebeard

It was late in March and freezing gales roared with exceptional violence. As the afternoon passed, sleet pasted the windows, casting a dull shade into the parlor. We sat on either side
of the fire. Gramm, sipping a cup of tea, gazing dreamily into
the leaping flames, and I, moodily twisting the antique locket
of gold that had rested around my neck for the past four years.
I was recuperating from an illness that had left me malinger-
ing. For a few weeks I was once again an occupant in the home
of my childhood, cosseting myself quite shamelessly.

"She was so lovely, so happy then," I sighed mournfully after
snapping the medallion open to gaze wistfully at the miniature
painting cupped in my hands. It showed a woman with sparkling
eyes and a generous mouth, Victoria, my twin sister. A tiny scroll
curled around a lock of auburn hair. *To my beloved sister,
Elizabeth,* it said.

"I remember taking the two of you to sit for these portraits.
That was before her marriage, of course," Gramm said with a
shaking voice.

Four years ago, Victoria had married a lighthouse keeper. As she prepared to follow him to Presque Isle station on Lake Huron, Gramm had commissioned a local artist to paint our individual portraits. She had purchased identical pendants for Victoria and me.

The tender love binding twins, these two kindred souls, is so strong that upon our tearful separation we vowed to always wear the ornament. My sister's pretty features had rested close to my heart ever since.

William Dougall had entered our lives as a fox penetrates a hen house: with greed and cunning. Oh, his bearded face was handsome enough, and his manners quite smooth, but his icy blue eyes and harsh face never fooled me. They shone branded by every evil passion. Victoria saw none of that, she bestowed on her fiancé the deepest affection. Our aged and feeble father had offered no objection to the marriage. Mother, upon her death, had left us a substantial dowry. The fox had married a "plump" maiden. For my sister's sake, I cast aside my doubts and wished them well, foolish enough to believe in the redeeming powers of a gentle woman.

Alas! A terrible change came over the bride within three years of the marriage. I don't know exactly why or what—Victoria did not mention it in her letters and I did not want to pry. But our thoughts had always been intimately linked, and I inferred certain distress. Her prose lacked the familiar vivacity, it conveyed a mysterious agitation, a disturbing uneasiness. Gone were the lively, gossipy little tidbits we'd always shared. *Dearest William* was barely mentioned or with such circumspection that a disquieting apprehension began to sweep over me.

How many times had I beseeched her to let me visit to receive a hasty, uneasy refusal veiled in thin excuses? I sensed a frightening, cold difference; this was not the fancy of a nervous, overly devoted woman. Victoria was definitely in a state of anguish—but my suspicions were so vague, so difficult to ascertain, that I dared not share them with anyone but Gramm. There I sat, my eyes closed, my body sunk in a plush armchair, reviewing the events which affected my sister, when Betty, our maid, entered the parlor.

"Ma'am," she said to Gramm. "There is a gentleman to see you. He insists upon talking to you immediately."

A man splattered with mud strode into the room. Such was the urgency of his mission that he had not bothered to discard his overcoat. Removing a dripping cap, he bowed to Gramm. "Captain Duffy. Pardon me, ma'am to intrude upon your privacy," he glanced briefly my way. "The matter is rather . . . delicate."

"Pray, speak freely," she admonished.

His face was so grim, so somber, that an immediate and terrible feeling of impending tragedy pressed upon me. "It's about Mrs. Dougall."

At my sister's name, I shot out of my chair, a trembling hand upon my heart.

Captain Duffy quickly explained that keeper Dougall was not aware of this visit and would probably disapprove of the invasion of his privacy, but my sister's situation alarmed the captain. In brief, Victoria seemed to be wasting away in the manner of one who is burdened by a heavy, dark secret.

"Mrs. Dougall is with child, you see." Again his eyes darted my way.

With child? Gramm and I exchanged hurt, astonished looks.

"No doubt my granddaughter has not had time to appraise us of the forthcoming event," my grandmother said quickly.

Captain Duffy shifted uncomfortably on his feet. "It is my belief that her time is coming soon." Stricken, I slumped back into my chair. Why, why had Victoria not told us?

"She begged me to give you this," Captain Duffy said, handing me a tattered piece of paper.

I read aloud, *"Come. Afraid."* Two words. Hastily scrawled on a torn page of a notebook, how heavy they bore on me! *Afraid,* she said. Afraid of having a baby? Afraid of what?

"You must go at once," Gramm insisted as soon as the man had departed. "Take the family Bible to enter the child's name."

Without notice, my bag packed, the precious Bible safely

tucked inside, I took the first ship going up Lake Huron and begged its captain to let me disembark at the light.

When we had parted, Victoria had been a cheerful, glowing bride. Now I stared at her with consternation and alarm. She had grown gaunt; hollow cheeks, eyes frightened like those of some hounded animal, and hair peppered with premature gray. Her expression as she greeted me was haggard and apprehensive. A meager bulge protruded from underneath a dull gown. Aghast, dreadful ideas ran through my head. What ghastly sickness was consuming her? Our reunion was tearful.

William's icy blue eyes flashed diabolically, his anger immediately squelched by a silky smile. A man of considerable strength with a bushy beard, he reminded me of Bluebeard, the killer of wives. An unpleasant sensation seeped into my heart. I stood a moment, wondering.

My ship brayed goodbye. A wave of panic washed over me. Alone with Bluebeard and my poor sister and not a single habitation for miles around! I followed the couple into their dwelling with trepidation.

The abode was comfortable and immaculately cleaned. It would have been cheerful but for the oppressing gloom that hung in the air.

How I longed to speak with my sister, to pamper her shrunken form into a healthy plumpness, to revel in the upcoming birth! Alas, William's sinister figure always loomed between us.

Victoria miserably avoided my questioning glances. In a state of nervous tension, I glanced uncomprehendingly at the couple. She was in such a guarded mood that I despaired of gaining her confidence and trust.

Bluebeard—*Bluebeard*, now why did that name keep popping up?—eyed me suspiciously. Unsettled by his shadowing of my every move, I fidgeted with my locket. The same anxiety remained with me throughout the evening.

Dinner was a silent, miserable affair. Victoria scurried about like a frightened mouse, refusing my help, casting weary glances at her husband. Once, in nervous haste, she smeared food upon the tablecloth. William swore a terrible curse. She visibly shrank from him. Aghast, I felt a repulsive notion seep into my brain. No, it could not be. Ridiculous.

My eyes sought my twin's. A startled cry escaped my lips. Never had I beheld such misery. A horrible muted appeal for help flared in her poor tormented eyes.

At last the unthinkable struck me.

William. Victoria was afraid of her own husband.

Trembling with anger and revulsion, I drew my breath hard to contain an outburst—confronting the loathsome beast would provoke greater wrath.

At last, with a warning scowl and a snarl, the detestable scoundrel flung his napkin on the floor and strode out to tend to his duties.

After his departure, my deathly pale sister crumbled on a rocking chair, shivering. I rushed to wrap a blanket round her drooping figure.

Brushing it aside, "It is not cold which makes me quake," she said in a fearful voice, tears glistening in her haunted eyes.

"Tell me," I pressed.

"Terror," she whispered between sobs. "Terror . . . another wo . . . woman. William, he, he . . ."

The door burst open. Bluebeard framed himself darkly in the aperture.

"Did I hear my name, my dear?"

Victoria hastily scrambled up. A loathing glare with a thinly-veiled threat pinned me in place. No talk, no confidence between the twins that evening. The husband saw to that.

I went to bed with a feverish mind, trembling with frustration and anger. The same two words rolled helplessly in my head. Another woman. Another woman. Did Victoria mean a mistress? And she with child! Obsessed with my sister's distress and scheming to end it, yet feeling powerless to intervene, I knew it would take me a long, long time to drift to sleep. Propped against my pillow, in the flickering candle amber glow, I sought solace in the Bible. My fingers lingered on the two names lovingly inscribed in Mother's bold writing, *Victoria and Elizabeth Henry, born September 18, 1823.*

A sudden outburst of uncontrollable male rage broke the silence of the night.

"Please don't go, don't go! Not her! Not her!" pled my sister in a voice quivering with abject suffering.

Heart throbbing, for a few seconds I sat with straining ears. *Her*. Did she mean the other woman or . . . me? A sickly shriek died on my frozen lips.

A whacking sound echoed through the house. Rage mingled with overwhelming fear for both of us jumbled my thoughts.

A ghastly, piercing scream made me shoot out of bed, Bible clasped to my heaving chest.

"Not the tower! Not the tower! Don't lock me there!"

Another whack, another ragged moan of pain, "No . . . don't go!"

The slamming of a door shook the walls. Footsteps coming my way! Bluebeard was after me! I frantically looked about the room for an exit, a place to hide.

There was no way out.

My door shook with a violent start. I stared at it with horror. Victoria stumbled in, her pallid face contorted with terror, hands groping her belly. She writhed in agonizing pain.

I had barely reached her when William's dissolute face appeared at the door. Blood froze in my veins; I was bereft of thought, incapable of movement.

With a terrible roar of "In the tower!" Bluebeard caught his terrified wife by the hair and begun to drag her out of the room. "Your turn next," he bellowed in my direction. At last my body jerked into action. It hurled itself at the monster. I fought as desperately and as powerlessly as one struggles with a wild beast.

Too late, I saw a fist and heard a swish—my vision blurred.

Why am I laying on the floor, my head throbbing and a viscous fluid trickling down my nose? It is dark, very dark. The place is deadly quiet. Where am I?

There burst forth the bloodcurdling screams of a terrified woman. Victoria's voice! Not in the house, but muffled by the stillness of the outside world. In a nightmarelike atmosphere, images—abominable images—flash back to me. The lighthouse! Bluebeard!

I grope wildly about me. Ah, my Bible!

Mindless terror makes me spring up. Hurry! Hurry! Flee from this cursed place and its demoniac keeper!

Victoria, where are you?

Bible in hand, I lurch outside and run madly, with no particular direction, nowhere to go but the lake and a black vastness of gnarled trees. Run, run, run! I keep running, stumbling and slipping on rocks and roots, invisible obstacles of doom, scrambling up and fleeing again.

Another terrible cry pierces the night. My eyes turn toward its source. The tower! There against the light of the lantern, two figures are struggling. This is no ordinary fight, but an obscene battle for life, for the right to fill one's lungs with wondrous cleansing air, to rock a baby to sleep, to love and be loved.

The larger shape raises one arm. A horrible scream of death reaches for the universe, crashes upon the moons and countless stars.

Victoria!

Deafened by hysteria, blood banging in my ears, mindless of my own safety, I put on a desperate burst of speed, Bible clasped against me like a shield. Just as I reach the foghorn building, Bluebeard emerges from the tower. I dart in the shadow of the small structure. He strides toward the house with a murderous countenance. He is going back for me!

Hurry! Hurry!

I scramble breathlessly up the echoing steely stairs, screeching, "I am coming darling! I am coming!"

I throw myself against the door of the lantern room. It bursts open. In his haste Bluebeard has not locked it! In the blinking light, an appalling sight meets my terrified eyes. My sister is lying on the floor in a pool of blood, her throbbing body covered with horrible wounds.

"Darling!" I cry in one big, racking sob.

A slight pulse in her neck tells me she is still alive. Her belly is terribly convulsed. The child! I sink next to her. My hands

flutter helplessly over her body; there is not a place that does not hurt, does not bleed. I don't know what to do except wipe her agonizing face with the hem of my nightgown, uttering incoherent prayers, words of love.

"Beth." Just a raspy murmur.

"I am here. Don't talk. You'll be all right." I lie, blinded by tears. Bluebeard will be back soon. Move! I reach for her prostrate figure.

One icy, bloody little hand stops me. "No . . . too late."

"I'll carry you, keep you safe." Wild, impossible promises burning my lips, cracking my heart.

"No!" she cries feebly between two harbored breaths. "Go— save yourself!"

"Never, darling, never," I sob against my wet palms.

"Wi . . . William, he locks me here . . . when he goes to . . ."

"I know, darling, save your strength."

"To . . . to . . ."

Her voice is fading, the pulse in her neck is slowing. I hear pounding footsteps in the yard. Quick, the Bible! Let it bring us a swift death and eternal peace!

Choked by tears, I fumble with the sacred book. My eyes stumble on the first page. *Victoria and Elizabeth Henry, born September 18, 1823.* I gasp. Blood freezes in my veins. In shock, I see the A from my sister's name fade and disappear, then the I, the T.

The circular stairs rattle under the thudding of approaching boots.

As the V dissolves, a faint sigh escapes Victoria's lips. "Goodbye darling" I whisper with all the loneliness of the world.

He's coming! The last three letters in my name vanish, then the B, the A . . .

He's here.

On the threshold of death, I am beyond terror.

Riveted in place, I see the arm raised, the glittering of a blade.

Presque Isle, which means "almost an island" in French, is a beautiful small peninsula, covered with fragrant cedars and pines, which pokes out into Lake Huron. Located between Port Huron and Michilimackinac, for centuries it has provided a perfect refuge for ships. It became even more popular in the 1830's when mariners began to use it as a source of cordwood for their greedy steamers. Prompted by increasing demand, Congress approved the building of a light. Old Presque Isle was erected in 1840 and closed in 1868 to build a taller light nearby. New Presque Isle was completed in 1871.

An old legend says that a keeper used to lock his wife in the tower when he visited his paramour. The poor woman was slowly wasting away of loneliness. One night, as she begged him not to lock her in the wind-battered tower, he killed her, silencing his wife for good. Or so he thought . . . Some folks claim that on certain nights the wails and desperate cries of the wretched woman can be heard riding the wind and crashing waves.

Reports differ as to which Presque Isle—the Old or the New— housed the murder. I chose to set my story in the first one only because the very distant past makes it more mysterious.

Rock of Ages, 1930
Isle Royale, Lake Superior

The Painting

Minnesota, 1930

Clickety, clack, clack, clack, went Emily and Elizabeth's knit-ting needles, setting rhythm to the two women's continu-ous prattling. Exasperated, Hester stood up abruptly, slamming her book shut.

"Where are you going?" squeaked her two sisters-in-law in unison.

"Hester! Continue reading," ordered her mother-in-law, eagle-eyed and dominant, from the depth of her bed.

Hester swallowed an angry retort and, summoning all her will, managed to sit in control of herself.

Since her return from nursing in the Great War twelve years ago—she'd gone to France and Belgium—she had held several private posts in that profession. Fiercely independent, passion-ate about privacy, she had roamed at will from state to state, thriving on self-sufficiency. She religiously deposited a good por-tion of her income at the bank for the day when she would buy a little cottage by the sea and call time her own.

The Wall Street Crash had cruelly altered her plans. All the money was gone; jobs became scarce. She had been forced to accept whatever positions became available, the last one, six months ago, calling her to the bedside of cantankerous Mrs. Mulligan.

In addition to two unmarried middle-aged daughters, the old tartar had a son, Arthur, who had "Upped and joined the Merchant Navy at a young age, and never got married," Mrs. Mulligan explained day after day.

"Really? I wonder why," always replied the nurse, not without irony.

The photograph by the bed showed a man with a stern face cut in two by a gigantic, protruding mustache, not unlike tusks; and whom Hester secretly called "The Walrus."

Whenever she could escape, Hester dashed to the library to avidly scan newspaper ads, always with the same devastating result: Nothing! Freedom. Peace. When would she ever enjoy them again? Disheartened, she returned to jail, for that's what the Mulligan household had become.

Then an unanticipated proposition cracked open the door of the dungeon, and while not opening to wide horizons, it promised a breath of fresh air.

At the age of fifty, Arthur retired from the Navy and returned home for an extended visit. He could barely stand listening to his sisters' insufferable bickering and his mother's constant wails. One month after arriving, Arthur Mulligan, whose general conversation included several variations of grunts similar to those of deep-sea mammals (Hester praised herself for nicknaming him so aptly) had applied for a position of lighthouse keeper, preferably to an isolated post.

A request from the Coast Guard Service, especially delivered by mail, made him frown. That same day, he proposed to Hester.

"Yes! Yes! Yes!" She cried petulantly to the tusks, grunts and all. A quiet man! On the grumpy side, but quiet all the same! A lighthouse keeper to boot, possibly on an island! Peace! The shouts, gushed out halfway through the proposal, had sent the "Walrus" reeling.

Years later, she learned that keepers had to be married to obtain a position. By then she did not care at all.

Not one whit in love, the pair courted blissfully, for each saw in the other the perfect solution to a personal objective. They exchanged contented looks.

One month later, to the disapproval of his family, the pair had tied the knot.

On their first night together, in the shadow of their cramped room—tucked between his sisters' and across from his mother's—Arthur flipped their nightshirts up, jerked his hips twice and gave one grunt that was supposed to satisfy them both.

Smothered under a hairy chest and a flabby belly, Hester had imagined better.

I'll just think of my lighthouse, she decided.

As the "one flip, two jerks, one grunt stint," as she came to call it, turned into a nightly ritual, she improved on the lighthouse. She added a sofa, a carpet here and there, and changed the print on the curtains. Two months later, her imagined lighthouse was so grand she burst into a brilliant smile.

"Mmm, good, wasn't it?" snorted Arthur, very pleased with himself.

"Yes. Just perfect," agreed his wife.

Oh, how Hester wished for her island with its pretty lighthouse! Every day, she clawed through the mail, searching wildly for the Coast Guard seal.

She had just returned from a walk in the early morning rain and was brushing the water off her hat, when the letter came.

She laughed with delight. Freedom at last! There was a radiance in her that sent Arthur reeling. They tore off the seal.

The post was Rock of Ages, near Isle Royale, on Lake Superior, fifty-four miles away from the nearest town, Port Arthur, Ontario; effective immediately. The pair exchanged a smug look. Peace at last!

The next line broke Hester's heart; air refused to reach her lungs. No women allowed, except for a two-week visit.

"It's a very small island, 150 feet at its longest point." Arthur coughed, a barely suppressed glimmer of triumph shining in his ordinarily placid eyes.

In one piercing moment, she knew then that he would accept the post and leave her behind. Marriage had been for naught! With perverse indifference, after requesting a spouse for their keepers, the Coast Guard was sending Arthur to one of the few posts for single men!

"They say it is the loneliest lighthouse in the nation," Arthur added sheepishly.

She looked at him long and levelly, too proud to cast herself on a chair and bawl her heart out. "Indeed. How convenient."

"I'll send for you soon," he promised, and went to pack, whistling.

Two months had passed, and here she was, still waiting. It was such an endless, depressing wait. Her heart threatened to break with the need for isolation, time to think; the tension was so great within her, she could not sleep.

"Girl! Keep reading!" Ordered the despot.

In the afternoon, she ran some errands and when she returned, three pairs of eyes bore through her accusingly.

On a silver tray, although addressed to her, lay an opened letter in Arthur's handwriting. She tore through it, noticing only a few words, "Come immediately. P.S. Bring your nursing bag."

Yes! At last.

The white lighthouse, with its blinking yellow eye, stood on a massive rock like a gigantic seagull. Engineers had had to blast the top of the island to build its cylindrical structure of steel plate and concrete. The conical tower and its watchroom stood 130 feet high, a warning of treacherous reefs, barely hidden under the surface of the lake.

Rock of Ages lighthouse, on the western side of Isle Royale, the side protected by the lee of that land, was built to mark a deadly peril—the Rock itself. The 150-foot long rock had so terrified mariners that, until the erection of the light, they had preferred to face the stormy waters of the eastern passage.

Hester's spirits had begun to revive with the arrival of the letter, but as the boat neared the island, she positively glowed. For once in a very long time, she would be alone. Her eyes caught sight of her husband waiting on the dock, all muffled up although it was a clear, pleasant day. Not quite alone, she sighed.

After a brief welcoming grunt, Arthur guided her to their circular, half-bare, one-room dwelling at the base of the tower. Not exactly the abode she had imagined but still, she would be free from the Mulligan women for two glorious weeks.

Arthur looked ghastly, ill-shaven and feverish. "Did you bring your nursing bag?" he coughed.

Pneumonia, she concluded after examining him and mixing some potions. "You need a doctor and someone to share your duties," she said through clenched teeth, suddenly understanding the purpose of the invitation.

She spent the first few days swallowing bitter tears, familiarizing herself with the light and its routine and coping with her sick husband's constant demands. "Hester, I am thirsty! I am hungry! The light! The signals! Quicker, woman!"

At night, from a makeshift pallet on the cold concrete floor, her thoughts turned to the distant past, when she had been mistress of her life, wondering if such happiness would ever return.

As Arthur worsened she took over all of his duties. On the fifth day, exhausted and disheveled, she gave up. She learned to use the radio and called for a replacement and a boat to take them to the mainland.

When the men from the freighter rowed ashore, "Keeper coming to relieve you soon, ma'am. Will have to make do until then," they said.

"But . . . I . . . I . . . My husband," she stammered.

"'Be all right."

Hester was too dazed by the news and its implications to comment wryly about the Great Establishment that approved or disapproved of women as need be. Could she credit her ears? Had her dreams come true? For the first time in years, no orders to obey, time would be her own. She reeled with the shock.

"Keep an eye on the lights and the signals!" Arthur cried feebly when they carried him away.

Hester passed her first day truly alone in a state of ecstasy, exploring the lighthouse, descending and ascending its interminable stairs cheerfully, her passion for solitude at last gratified. She stood on the platform, listening to the quivering of the light, whistling wind, pounding rain and the clicking of the gears.

At first she ate, worked and slept as she pleased, but as days went by and no freighter stopped by with a replacement, work and sleep came round with an irritating regularity.

A week later, the novelty of her newly-found solitude wore off. Work turned monotonous, log-keeping routine. Her mind had run out of daydreams. That afternoon she tore strips of an old skirt and spent hours decorating the island's only brush with printed bows.

The following morning she discovered a stack of white paint and brushes. Scampering barefoot across the rock, an old sheet wrapped around her midriff, she bent here and there to clumsily dab blobs and lines at the gray stone. Hester had no artistic bend, and it showed. By the end of the day, she'd run out of paint and space, and the rock—as if attacked by a band of unruly children—resembled a wild and disorderly playground, its big white blobs a cross between a zebra and a Dalmatian.

That night she fancied there was some peculiarity in the cylindrical walls; the beating of her heart pulsated strangely in the tower and its steel stairs. She began to feel uneasy about her isolation. She lay awake, listening, and waiting for she did not know what, remembering that the coast had always had a bad name.

"Alone!" she whispered, and how that word filled her with horror! Oh, to hear another voice, to see another face!

Hester mounted to the platform to gaze at approaching fog, a whitish blanket unfurling itself over the lake, gobbling its black, velvety water.

"Alone! I don't want to be alone anymore! I want company! Company! Company!" she shouted about.

The fog closed around the light.

That night, she sat rigidly on her bed, readying herself for danger.

She had just dozed off when a sudden crashing noise woke her up like some horrible nightmare. Stumbling outside, her eyes fastened to an enormous, looming black shape bulging out of the inky water. The freighter—it was a freighter, not a monster as she had crazily feared for a moment—had struck a submerged rock and was evidently damaged; it seemed to stand right on end. Someone lit a flare, and from its red, pallid glow, she saw men fall overboard puppetlike. She realized the wreck was too far to cast a line and that many lives depended on her following action. Stupefied for a brief moment, she imagined the men drowned and their bodies washed up at her feet. Quick! Move!

She scrambled her way to the rowing boat attached to the dock, threw in coils of lines and the six life jackets kept there for emergencies and launched into the night. Pure madness!

She heard men shouting, red flares burning. Men everywhere! In the water, swimming wildly; on the wreck, lowering lifeboats. She plucked six of them from the water and rowed them ashore. The hull creaked and heaved, hurling ten more into the water. Thank goodness they all had life belts! They swam to the shore, helped pull others from the frigid water.

Hester scoured the light surf, looking for injuries. One man had a crushed leg, another a broken arm. On her seventh trip, a man leapt from the bridge into her boat, holding tightly a canvas bag in one hand and a wooden box in the other. He clung to them as if his very life depended on their safety. "My paintings!" he shouted to Hester through a golden mane pasted to his face.

She and the men worked for hours and saved 125 lives. At last, the captain reported every one was safely ashore. "Every one?" She cried incredulously.

One hundred and twenty-five men sheltered in a thirty-foot diameter lighthouse. The place, so empty before, was packed with shivering sailors. Men, their voices echoing on the steely walls, piled on the bed, the table, the trunk, the stairs and in the watchtower until not one inch was available.

Hester, who hours before had begged for company, desperately tried to collect her wits. Dazed, she attended to the injured as best she could, groping her way through the throng, stumbling over stretched legs. The captain radioed for help.

During the night, as the men dropped off to sleep, the temperature rose and the air became stale.

At sunrise, the painter with the golden hair, Giono Bellini, stepped outside to breathe the clean air. He was an Italian who had traipsed across America for the previous four years to capture its wilderness on canvas and in obscure and long-winded poems that even his devoted mother did not read.

The first thing that caught his eyes was Hester's handiwork, those white blobs defiantly clinging to the gray rock. "Belle! Belle!" he exclaimed enthusiastically, already half in love with its creator, man or woman, single or not. Giono, his curls bleached golden by the sun and wind, his soul full of romantic notions, was a poet and an artist, not a gifted one, but extremely prolific. He accepted no financial rewards for his considerable work nor, in fact, had any ever been offered by friends and relatives. This fact did not disturb his beautiful blond head. Giono grandly bestowed his work on bewildered recipients who accepted them in hapless dismay. His pictures cluttered more attics than any of his fellow painters.

He was an idealist and strikingly handsome.

He was also single and wealthy.

He had been staring at the white drawings when Hester popped out for a bit of fresh air. "Pretty bad, isn't it?" she smiled.

"You are the artist?" His voice quaked with admiration.

Hester took a startled breath.

Giono's eyes lingered upon her face. Her black curls had cascaded upon her shoulders, framing her weary but handsome features in a glorious disorder. Giono Bellini thought he was dreaming. At last, on that most unlikely spot, came the woman he had been waiting for, specially molded to his fantasy, a fellow painter, an artist, and a goddess.

With that thought, he walked with a palpitating heart to

Hester. "Marry me!" he cried as an introduction. "I must have you, love you. I'll paint you in the Botticelli style—nude with your magnificent hair as a single ornament; honey blond curls, eyes sea-blue."

Under her ebony curls, Hester's brown eyes clouded. She was reduced to incoherence. "W . . . What?"

"Marry me! We both have talent and beauty! We'll make splendid babies!" Bellini took her hand and kissed it passionately. "I have wealth, let me share it with you!" He declared in an unabashed bid for happiness. His voice was low-pitched, as smooth as Chianti under olive trees on a lazy afternoon.

For a moment, Hester, completely dazed, said nothing, just stared at the golden man dropping to his knees. Should she laugh or call for help? The beautiful face across from her was serious. After a while, bereft of words, "Oh," was all she could utter.

Insane? Eccentric? Possibly both, but Giono knew what he wanted. Undeterred, "Marry me! Come to Tuscany, we'll make love by the sea!" he promised.

That his smooth voice and graceful body promised more than two jerks and one grunt was obvious. "I already have a husband," said Hester with a touch of regret.

"Leave him! You are made for me," said the gorgeous form at her feet.

Stunned, she ran into the lighthouse on legs she never knew she had. Giono was hard at her heels. "I must marry her!" he shouted to the captain.

"Maybe you should speak of that another time," coughed the poor man.

Giono stood in the doorway, gazing after Hester, completely besotted.

In the evening, a freighter arrived with relief. Arthur was sitting in a rowboat coming ashore, all muffled up and a cane in one hand.

"What . . . what? He cried, turning purple upon noticing Hester's rock painting. "You'll have to clean that up, girl. All of it," he grunted in guise of welcome.

"Are you the lady's husband? She is not for you, you know," declared Giono Bellini without a trace of malice. "I must marry her, must have her. You have to let her go."

Arthur stood stock-still, staring at him.

"You do not appreciate her voluptuous body and glorious hair. She's made for love." His gaze dropped to Arthur's stocky shape with perfect horror. "She needs a beautiful man," said Giono as a final argument. He turned sweetly to Hester. "Come, you will be my muse. Together, we'll paint a radiant world!"

Hester's eyes darted between the two men in confusion. Smothering a cry, she fled to the light.

"Now, see what you have done!" Protested the suitor indignantly to the speechless husband.

Seconds later, Hester scrambled to the shore. She hurled starched aprons and nursing bag into the lake. "Bye bye, Arthur!" she shouted gaily, free at last.

"What about my health? My mother, my sisters?" wailed her husband.

She jerked her hips twice and grunted once. "They're all yours!"

Turning to Giono, "Tuscany you said?"

Giono nodded charmingly.

"Come, then," she said, taking the hand of her golden Adonis.

She did not live happily ever after, but she had lots of fun.

The Rock of Ages light, near Isle Royale, is one of the most isolated on the Great Lakes. It was built in 1908 to warn captains of a deadly peril—the rock itself.

Even so, on a foggy day, in May 1933, the freighter *George Cox* rammed into the nearby reefs, and its 125 passengers and crew were shipwrecked. Keeper John Soldenski helped rescue the 125 survivors who took refuge inside the light tower, packed like sardines until another ship took them to the mainland.

The light cannot be seen from any shore, but can be glimpsed from the decks of the ferries that carry visitors from Grand Portage, Minnesota, to Isle Royale.

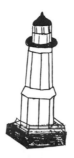

Grosse Ile North Channel Light, 1998
Detroit River

Genuine Concern

One momentary lapse in concentration, that's all it took Jack Marden. And his life changed forever.

When it happened, he was exhausted, a real bundle of nerves. The transatlantic flight from Amsterdam to Metro Detroit had been crowded. He'd been squeezed in the middle row (the one he'd specifically requested Not-To-Be-Seated-At). For hours he sat between a couple of businessmen arguing over sales strategy and a little old lady snoring over four brandies. Violent turbulence had kept safety belts fastened for most of the time, he'd already seen the movie, and a kid two rows behind had bawled throughout the flight. Definitely not one of the best.

He should have taken a taxi and returned to the airport for his car after a good nap. At least the trip had been very successful, which made up for the flight. Jack grinned. Automatically his gaze dropped to the maroon briefcase protruding slightly from under the seat. He had managed to purchase fifty million dollars worth of diamonds, just in time for the San Diego trade show where he expected to make a handsome profit.

When the girl with the black suitcase stepped in front of his car, a big yawn was stretching his mouth. He was thinking it was too late to deposit the case in the bank vault, he would put it in his office instead. By the time he slammed a foot on the brake, it was too late. "Oh, God!" he cried as a thud shook the front of his vehicle and a lithe body was catapulted puppetlike across the hood.

It was such a terrible shock that for a brief instant he was petrified. The girl hunched over her hands, which dangled at odd angles; her hair was torn and her face contorted with pain. She alternately moaned and cried.

He shot out of his car, instinctively grabbing his briefcase. The safety of his package was second nature to him; he'd been a diamond dealer for too long.

"Someone call 911!" he yelled at random to the bystanders already dawdling around the scene of the accident. "Get a doctor! Get an ambulance!" He turned frantically to his victim: "You'll be okay, miss! Help is coming! Don't move!" Don't touch her, he reminded himself, it might be fatal.

A police car pulled up and two men got out. "The ambulance is on its way," one of them stated while the other somberly requested documents and a statement. Still shaken by the trauma, Jack docilely answered all questions in a subdued voice. Better cooperate, the situation looked bad enough as it was. Between harried answers, he peeped nervously over one shoulder to watch the ambulance come to an abrupt stop and the medics dash to give assistance.

After what seemed like an eternity, but must have been only a few minutes, the officer let him go. He received several additional points, a stiff fine, and an order to report to the precinct within twenty-four hours for a full investigation.

The ambulance women were very efficient. In a matter of seconds, still conscious, she was hooked to an assortment of tubes and other medical paraphernalia. Jack rode with her. Bending anxiously over her pale face, high cheekbones and generous lips, he thought she looked teasingly familiar. Then he remembered. Of course! The woman from the snack bar across from the dealer in Amsterdam where he'd sipped some coffee before the meeting. Must have been in the same plane.

Her name was Gertrude Vanderoot and she had no relatives, she mumbled through ragged breath, her mouth shaking with the effort. Today was the first day of her vacation after saving for two years for the trip. Damn!

The waiting at the hospital was awful. There was very little for him to do, except worry about the future, a terrible guilt resting on his shoulders. How serious were the injuries? Did she have insurance? What if she died? His eyes clouded and he slumped on a hard sofa for a long time, head sunk in his hands. Why had not he paid closer attention?

"Mr. Marden?"

He lifted his gaze to a tired-looking young doctor, who explained the young woman's condition. For some unknown reason—various tests and X-rays were fine—both of Gertrude's hands were damaged; they did not respond to stimulation and required more tests. She had no U.S. insurance, and Jack had accepted to foot the bill. He simultaneously felt relieved that she was alive and tormented over two tragically useless hands.

The doctor advised him to go home; Gertrude was medicated and fast asleep, maybe for ten to twelve hours.

Jack took a taxi back to his car and drove to his immaculate Victorian home on Grosse Ile, a gorgeous, charmingly old-fashioned island located in the Detroit River before it pours into Lake Erie. He was too exhausted to dash to his office and lock the brilliants in the safety box.

The night was a nightmare. He tossed and turned, alternately hot and cold, until he finally fell in a fitful sleep in the early hours of the morning. By the time he woke up, the bank was closed—on Saturdays it opened only for a few hours. He directed his car toward the office and realized he had forgotten the keys. Cussing, he lugged his valuable bundle to the hospital.

Gertrude looked better, if a little wan, and bravely swallowed sobs over her limp hands resting loosely on the blanket. She flashed a glance at the case clasped in his fingers. Automatically, Jack tensed his hold, and instantly felt foolish. What could the poor girl do? Snatch it with a foot and hop down the corridor?

"I don't want to stay here," she whimpered with an engaging Dutch accent after he had humbly apologized repeatedly with obvious sincerity (and anxiety). "I have bad memories of hospital, too much of it when I was a child." She raised big imploring eyes. "I just need a break, will come back for the tests."

He looked at her steadily. His mind quickly decided. This was the only decent thing to do. "Look here, I am an adaptable sort of fellow . . . I have a proposition; it's a bit unusual, please don't take offense, but under the circumstances . . ." He paused for a moment. "Come to my house. I'll look after you."

Gertrude had listened, at first amazed, then fascinated, a curious light shooting up her eyes. A faint specter of suspicion wafted through Jack's mind, but he quelled it as soon as it popped into his head. She smiled quizzically, fixedly. "No, thank you. I could not possibly accept . . ."

Although the girl's queer expression awoke a certain uneasiness, Jack clicked his tongue with irritation. He had harbored the notion that she would accept gratefully; it would ease his conscience and maybe avoid a lawsuit, a kind of buy out. "Look, here—I'm housetrained and have no fleas . . ."

She burst into shrill laughter. It hurt Jack's ears.

On the way to Grosse Ile, she asked about the place, excited about the prospect of staying on it, and marveled at the big body of water flowing from one Great Lake to another. She wore a yellow scarf Jack had tied over her hair. Once or twice he caught her glimpsing curiously at the case again stored under the driver's seat.

Jack's house stood on the island's water edge, two houses from the recently restored lighthouse.

"Oh, how quaint! A lighthouse!" She exclaimed, glancing at the white octagonal wooden structure. "Can we visit it?"

"What about your hands, don't they hurt?" Jack asked curtly.

Gertrude's girlish mannerisms were becoming vastly annoying.

"They don't hurt. Just refuse to work. Remember?" She snapped through pinched lips, staring pointedly at clawlike fingers.

Jack's teeth grated with the effort to control a burst of temper, but he was too full of remorse and fear to let go. There was a pause during which he savagely cursed himself for a damned fleeting concentration deficiency. The arrangement was not going to be easy.

Swallowing bitterness, "Don't you want to rest, see your room?" he suggested hopefully.

Gertrude pouted. Her companion privately thought that sulks, whilst charming on the face of little girls, were rather ugly on women.

"All right," he said none too gently. "Today is your lucky day. It's open to the public every weekend. We have to cross my neighbor's property to get to it."

He parked the car, hoisted her helpless form out of it, locked the doors and dumped the keys in one pocket. For once he abandoned caution and left the diamonds inside the vehicle.

As they crossed the manicured lawn, Jack saw a member of the Historical Society running the light on tour duty chatting with the house owner. He did not bother hailing her; they trusted him.

"Oh, Jack, let's go up, please!" Gertrude pleaded fervently— her wolfish smile widening. For the first time, Jack felt a chill race through his body.

They stood on the parapet, Jack pointing at landmarks, explaining historical details the way one does to foreign visitors. Forty feet above water, they stared at the blue water lapping at the broad concrete foundation. No freighters were in sight.

"Oh. My scarf!" Gertrude suddenly cried.

From a corner of one eye, Jack saw it floating over the rail. It all happened too fast for him to wonder how it had become undone. He simply leaned to catch it. Just as the tips of his fingers felt the soft material, one female hand slipped inside his pocket to retrieve the keys. As he plunged to his death, he recalled the imprint of two hands on his back.

Grosse Ile Lighthouse stands forty feet high on the east side of the island on the Detroit River. The island itself has retained a delightful historic flavor, definitely enhanced by the presence of the restored wooden tower.

The original light was erected in 1894 on three wooden legs; now it rests on a broad concrete foundation. When the Coast Guard decommissioned it in 1963, the Grosse Ile Historical Society raised the funds to purchase their landmark.

It is opened to the public. However, a member of the Historical Society must accompany visitors since the only access to the light is through private property.

Crisp Point Light
Lake Superior, Michigan

It

How long it had lived there, it could not say, only that stars are old, earth filled with secrets, nights bright and days are dark.

"Come to me," the land had whispered.

Awakened from a deep sleep, all cold and stiff, it had emerged from a solitude of water to a black world of sunshine.

To a place of no return.

It had slithered blindly, painfully, over sand and rocks, yesterday and today, and slipped into the brightness of a hollow of a round wall.

So hidden in the base of a turret, it had listened to words of love, of children squalling, or a woman's soothing voice, and the weary feet of the father coming home.

The moon had bent its amber face to trickle food without a name, light without warmth, to the viscous creature below.

How it envied the forbidden, dazzling rays that caressed children at play!

But dusk belonged to it, diffusing soothing vibrations from the world above.

111

Sounds, not gurgling, gagging ones emitted by land-living things when entering an alien, watery world, but soft murmurs, booming laughter and gentle lullabies had dripped from aloft.

It had gobbled happiness, hunger satiated by bliss, sight restored by twilight.

But ephemeral the voices must be, because they all disappeared.

Silence. Emptiness. Solitude.

Alone for long, long years in an abandoned dwelling place, remembered but by a few.

How dare birds sing, when immured in loneliness, stubborn hope grapples long and hard with despair?

This is the land washed by the sun, kissed by the breeze. Water rustles, not so far, yet unattainable.

Raspy, gossipy stones locked in decay whisper of a distant past, of a realm it had known. Interspersed with gangly weeds, old widows basking on a porch with little else to do, they hold sunshine in their withered bodies.

A tattered heart, something keeps it beating, something holds its hope. It listens for voices riding the wind, too soft to hear, too far to reach.

Will human beings ever come back here?

Prior to the erection of a light in 1904, many vessels on their way to Whitefish Point lost their bearing and crashed at Crisp Point, a wind-battered, isolated section of land that juts into Lake Superior. The station included a tower, keeper's dwelling, foghorn building and several outbuildings, but all that remains is the foundations of old docks and a beacon in dire need of repair. The light was abandoned to decay since being put out of service in 1989.

Fortunately for lighthouses enthusiasts, the Crisp Point Historical Society is in the process of restoring this threatened historical edifice. The station stands a few yards from the blue water on an unbroken stretch of sandy beach on a background of undulating dunes, a real treat for visitors.

Nottawasaga Island Light, 1995
One of the Imperial Towers, Georgian Bay, Canada

The Perfect Match

"**D**amn!" I muttered under my breath as a speedboat neared the island. The odds of having company on rugged Nottawasaga Island are so small it's what attracted me to the place. Most people avoided its lethal shoals.

"Hiiiiii!" The man cut the motor off and cautiously approached the lakeshore, watching his depth. "Hello there!" he shouted again in that abominable cheerful voice so distinctive of tourists. His companion, a woman, waved gaily.

Blast! With a sinking feeling, "Hello," I replied frostily to discourage further familiarity.

I had been commissioned to paint the six Imperial Towers by the family of a wealthy invalid who could no longer trot across the Great Lakes to visit lighthouses. This series of oils was a surprise for her ninetieth birthday. In the beginning of June, I had rented a houseboat, loaded my luggage, camera and pads and began drawing and photographing the splendid whitewashed stone sentinels to paint them later in my studio.

Nottawasaga had been kept to the last. It presided proudly and defiantly on a treacherous rock surrounded by gorgeous aquamarine water, a special challenge to my artistic talents. Indeed, most of the previous night had been spent devising new mixes, brilliant hues for the sky and lake.

The man reached for his companion. Both waded to the shore, he confidently, she hesitatingly, visibly clinging to his suntanned arm. They made a striking couple—young with good looks, an air of self-confidence, of people enjoying all the gifts that good fortune could bestow—money, power and charm. She was petite, graceful, with long blond curly hair framing her creamy skin and soft hazelnut eyes.

"Hi again. I'm John, this is my wife Goldie," said the man, showing two rows of perfect teeth that must have cost a fortune.

"I'm Anna," I conceded through tight lips, unwilling to be charmed and show uneven teeth.

A cellular phone poked out of his shorts pocket, which caused my hands to clench in deep aggravation. Peace and quiet, that's what the island was about; here were some city folks contaminating the area with noise and moneyed arrogance.

My voice had carried enough displeasure, because the young woman hastily clarified, "We won't disturb you. We're just stopping for a picnic." She looked shy, almost ill at ease, cocking her head at a queer angle. Her beautiful gentle eyes vaguely rested on me, a foot above my head. That's when I noticed that their softness was in fact a lack of focus, of expression.

She was blind and it made her look even more appealing.

It melted some of my resentment, "I'm an artist, sketching the light to paint it later," I said, explaining my chilly reception.

"You have a wonderful voice, firm with a hint of warmth. Lovely." One hand extended to my face and fluttered over it, learning its planes and contours. Surprised, I stiffened.

"Don't mind me," she said softly. "Strong features, nice bone structure. What color are your eyes? Eyes tell so much about a person . . . I used to see . . ."

"They're chestnut brown with a sparkle of gold," John answered before I could reply.

"Lovely. Eyes of an artist observe beyond shapes and motion, they witness life. I like that." There was a little smile in her words, as if she were secretly amused.

"Come on, darling. Let's leave Anna in peace." John carefully tugged his wife's arm, caressing it without thinking. "I'll sit you on a rock by the light and go get our stuff."

Love between them was so visible, so forcefully present that my glance dropped to my sandals in mild self-consciousness.

They settled by the lapping water, not very far from me. I tried to ignore them, to concentrate on my task; it was useless. Somehow the couple was always in my line of vision, foraging in their cooler or talking on their infernal phone in an excited sort of way. Words did not actually reach my ears, only petulant vibrations.

Suddenly John pocketed the cellular. After a brief conversation with Goldie, they feverishly collected their belongings, haphazardly throwing items in cooler and basket. They were going. At last!

Goldie seemed gloriously happy, exuberantly so. There was a reckless bounce in her step. "We're going back to town!" She shouted gaily, obviously bursting with some news.

"Tell her. Tell her!" John encouraged.

Words, shrill and excited, bubbled out of her mouth. "We've found a donor! I'm having a transplant! I'm going to see!"

Her elation was contagious. "That's wonderful! Here, take this." Rashly, I tore off the top page of my pad, "a memento of an extraordinary moment. The lighthouse for when your sight is restored."

She thanked me in a half-amused, half-ashamed way. John looked curiously at me. It felt queer.

Loaded like mules, they traipsed back to their boat. The motor coughed a few times, John was playing with the choke. It sputtered a couple more time and went dead.

I gritted my teeth, knowing what was coming.

"Eh, you! Anna! Can you tow us back?"

"Thanks ever so much, Anna. Let us buy you dinner," John said after docking.

"Thanks but . . ."

"We insist. To celebrate," added Goldie in the voice of a young woman who is used to getting her way.

My hackles went up; the tone did not please me. Besides, the afternoon gone, now an evening's work was threatened.

"You're in a hurry. The transplant—" I began cuttingly.

"Tomorrow. We're leaving first thing in the morning. We'll pack tonight," Goldie butted in. She seemed on edge; no doubt on account of the momentous event about to happen in her life.

John's eyes wandered to me with a sort of apprehension, as if hurt lest I refused. "Let's compromise. A drink, then," he said charmingly.

"Okay." One hour maximum I promised myself.

A curious smile flitted on Goldie's face. It puzzled me.

John jauntily grabbed my arm and his wife's. "We live close by. I'll fix us some Margaritas."

The atmosphere of the villa felt strangely chilled though there was mellow evening sunshine outside. A dank smell of alkali or some caustic disinfectant prickled my nose. A certain tension, similar to the agitation one suffers in the waiting room of a dentist, crept over me. There was a peculiarity in the air which I could not fathom.

"I'm a surgeon," said John, smiling in a most inscrutable way, "always fiddling with new chemicals. My hobby."

A harsh and sick laughter burst from Goldie's lips.

Utterly bewildered, I darted uncomprehending glances from one to the other.

Something was happening, the nature of which escaped my understanding. Unexplainably, blood banged in my ears, I felt a positive and uncomfortable tingling in my toes.

"Private joke," said John in quite a dry, different tone. He waved a hand at me. "Sit down. Be at ease."

I sat clumsily and bit my lips, peeping uneasily behind me into the corners of the room.

John mixed the drinks. "To sight!"

"To sight, the most beautiful gift!" Goldie giggled insanely as she spoke.

"To sight!" I joined in weakly, raising my glass with a jerky movement. Why were my fingers trembling so?

An awkward silence fell in the room.

Goldie curled on the sofa, suddenly serious. "Thank you, Anna." The timbre in her voice held genuine emotion.

"Don't mention it; it was just a tow."

"To me, it's more than that," she said cryptically.

I kept starting at every sound and forced myself to smile. Disturbing thoughts hovered on the edge of my consciousness. The room seemed suddenly smaller, I felt trapped.

John was behind a tall bar mixing another drink, I suppose. His brows knitted as though thinking deeply. "So, Anna. Are you in good health?"

The question was so ridiculously rude and inappropriate that for a few seconds I stared in shock. "Well, are you?" he asked with bizarre persistence.

A dark sense of dread, a vague premonition of evil struck me. I shuddered uncontrollably.

Goldie was again feverishly excited, borderline hysterical.

My mind froze, I gave a ghastly little shriek. I was afraid and became aware of my thumping heart as the fear turned to terror. "I must go," I cried thinly, tossing my drink aside and making for the door.

My legs buckled under me, I swayed and slumped back in the chair, looking wildly, fuzzily, around the dancing room. Through a cottony haze, I saw Goldie, an obscene, greedy smirk on her face. My body became heavy, tired and spongy.

I felt myself grasped; John had leapt from his position and was applying a pad over my mouth and nose. I struggled weakly, tried to scream; nothing came out of my muted mouth. I held my breath till I turned faint and my body gasped for air in a bid for preservation.

All went black.

Where am I? Why am I so cold? Why is everything so dark? I am drowsy, floating, seem to emerge from a long, long sleep. A sickly smell of chemicals mixed with blood and fear fill my nostrils.

My body is shaking feverishly, aches everywhere, especially my head which does not respond to any of my commands. My

skin is itching from the coarse fabric covering me. Come on, open your eyes, move your hands, your feet. Do something.

I can't! I can't! What is stopping me?

My breathing accelerates, my eyelids burn, panic fills my lungs.

Something very cold is dripping down my face; it feels like melting ice under a tight blindfold. My hand tries to reach it, identify it. I struggle to move. With a sob, I realize that I am strapped to a flat surface, some sort of a cot, by what feels like electrical cord wound around my ankles, my hands and my chest.

I lie there for a time, whimpering, terrified, straining against my bounds, against the unfamiliar, complete darkness surrounding me. A nameless horror fills me. "Help . . . Help . . ." The cry is pitifully weak.

"Hello, Anna."

Goldie! "Goldie where are you? Help me . . . Help me . . ."

"Hello, Anna," repeats the voice. "This is a voice-activated tape recording. An ambulance is coming; John sent an anonymous call to 911. We're on our way to the transplant. Thank you for the gift. You were so gullible, so easy, fell for the motor trick. John reckons your eyes are a perfect match for me. I wonder if I'll ever paint?"

Nottawasaga Light was erected in 1848 two miles from Collingwood Harbor to warn mariners of the lethal shoals surrounding the island. The whitewashed tower flashes against a wonderful setting of aquamarine water.

In 1959 a spark from the stove pipe set fire to the keeper's dwelling. The light was then converted to acetylene gas. It is now operated by a battery-powered light bulb charged by solar panel and blinks every ten seconds.

Ravaged once by fire, the old house fell into the hands of vandals who forced their way into the tower and tossed rocks through the crumbling roof, finishing what the blaze had started. The dwelling is now in ruins.

The island has been overtaken by weeds and poison ivy and is now home to several species of birds.

To Mike Gillespie: Thanks for the twisted idea and its appropriate title.

Waugoshance, 1871
Straits of Mackinac

Matey

No—it could not be.

Red's still head lay at an odd angle, frozen in endless sleep.

No customary wake up bark had stirred Allan that morning. It was the unusual silence that had aroused him from slumber.

Stricken, keeper Allan Quirt ran a desolate hand over his fourteen-year-old mongrel. He should have seen it coming. Old Red had acted strange lately—tired, not much interest in food and games. He had licked his master's fingers adoringly last night before lying in a loose ball with the jerky and hesitant motions of arthritic old age. Allan sighed deeply, sadly remembering a peculiar radiance in the dog's gentle eyes, the serene glow of one dying, sensing eternal rest has come at long last.

For twelve years they'd kept lights together, the last four at Waugoshance. Red acted as a companion, alarm clock and emergency warning. Man and hound had been inseparable—as if the two had been linked by an invisible thread. Up and down the cylindrical tower, along the short pier, in the lifeboat, wherever they were, Allan's hand used to stray about dreamily, sure to find a silky head under his palm. At three, Red had been dubbed "Matey" after warning the keeper of impending danger, storms and fog, with a queer throaty bark—emergency calls, as Allan was to describe them—way before any visible signs.

A sociable yap greeted schooners passing by, the dog running up and down the short pier with excitement. Ever popular with seamen, "Hello, Matey! Good boy!" The lookouts would shout from the crow's nest.

Fourteen years of unshakable affection, and now, silence. And loneliness.

Allen tore up an old sheet and began to sew it as a sack.

Old Red would receive a sea burial.

He deserved it; besides, the light and recent pier were all concrete, no chance of digging a grave there. Supported by a crib filled with stone, the conical brick structure sat on a treacherous shoal only twelve feet under. It protected mariners passing through the Straits from the shallow and perilous formation extending several miles into Lake Michigan.

After a brief but meaningful prayer, Red's body was sailed past the rock barrier and entrusted to the depths of the Lake.

A hush settled over the tower—one Allan, try as he might, could not adjust to. The missing was terrible. Sunrise had lost its glow, the pier was deserted, and solitary footsteps resonated with loneliness on the steely stairs. How often had he stretched a hand, to caress a dreadful emptiness? Vessels plowed by and shouts of "Where's Matey?" added to his misery.

It was then, three weeks from being relieved of his duty, a great fire blazed up in Chicago, casting a crimson trail of leaping tongues at the glowing sky. The flames kept rising and dancing like ghastly demons dissipating evil vengeance upon civilization. Lake and wind, tireless villains, began to swell, splash and roar, pushing a wall of ashes horizontally.

In hours, Lake Michigan was swallowed up in a murky shroud. Waters and lighthouse were imprisoned in a coffin of impenetrable darkness. Visibility was close to nil. Ships began to drift, blundering through a pea-soup fog. There was a bedlam of hands frantically yanking fog whistles, voices hysterical with fear, "We're going to be hit!" Men on schooners screamed in horror on bridges as vessels loomed menacingly over each other. "Abandon Ship!"

Night came, adding to the terror. Devoured by darkness, the Straits resembled a lost world, a nightmarish scene of cruel chaos, a somber and unbidden graveyard. Errant ships sounded pitiful wails as they crossed one another unseen, watchmen straining to probe the frightening obscurity. Several collided in an awful rasping, grating of splitting wood, spilling their wealthy cargo in a watery tomb. A few, the lucky ones, limped blindly in the unknown, while others stood their gaping belly right on end, hurling seamen into the inky and frigid gloom. Wild with fright and pain, sailors' ghostly forms clung to rafts in a desperate and uneven struggle with the current. Men disappeared, swept overboard and drowned, never to be found. Vessels sank, taking with them half-crazed hands trapped in their belly.

For long hours, certain that the flashing of the beacon could hardly penetrate the thick gray smog that clogged doors and windows, Allan continued jerking the foghorn rope every two minutes. A prisoner in his tower, with no one to assist him, he pulled and tugged. He listened, horror-stricken, to the slashing of hulls and ripping of sails and to the lonesome ships creeping, phantomlike, through hell.

Ten hours of misery, of standing and yanking, had twisted his muscles and cramped his fingers; a dreadful feeling of helplessness kept him blowing the horn. Shirt clammy with dank sweat, already aching with exhaustion, the poor fellow agonized over the lives that would be lost that night. Lives whose safety rested on his throbbing shoulders and weary mind. His brows knitted with anguish—when would this ordeal end? More to the point, how much longer could he stay awake? Allan rubbed his red-rimmed eyes and massaged his shoulders to release some tension.

By the clock it was sunrise. There was no improvement in the air, black had given way to choking grayness, but sight was still impossible. Allan was drunk with fatigue, swaying on numb feet. He could have dragged a chair and rested between blasts, but he was afraid of going to sleep and letting go of the line.

Except for three chamber pot dashes and a quick grab of sustenance, by midday, the keeper had not left his grueling post. A giant sepulcher of ashes still engulfed the lake in darkness. By mid-afternoon, disheveled and disoriented, Allan had tied the cable round his wrist and was tottering like a puppet in the wind. Later, he gave up and slumped on a chair. Humming tunelessly, he was valiantly fighting sleep yet could feel himself losing the battle. His body, his eyes, were heavy, so very heavy and heavier still. They closed.

The Marilyn fumbled in the gloom under shortened sails. Tossed about by cruel currents, she hesitantly approached the Straits, her lookout nervously peering into the vast nothingness ahead. The Navigating Officer bent over charts and compass, a furrow of deep concentration on his forehead.

"Heave the lead!"[1] Ordered Captain Weymour over one shoulder.

The leadsman pulled up the fathom line and counted. "By the mark, seven!"[2]

The captain relaxed a bit, with that kind of depth, they were clear of the shoal. He turned to the helmsman: "Steady on your heading."[3]

She was eight hundred yards from the light and aiming straight for it.

And getting closer.

---

[1] Depth sounding
[2] A fathom measures 6 feet
[3] Keep the same course

Unaware of impending danger, head slumped on his chest, Allan dozed. The room was unbearably stuffy and silent, yet a certain agitation, a flurry of emotions, a feeling of intense force prevailed within its cylindrical walls.

A draught blew in under the door. Suddenly, an earsplitting din exploded near Allan. Jolted awake and befuddled, he stared for a moment at his tied wrist. An abrupt noise had woken him up. He was not sure what kind, save that it was vaguely frightening, oddly familiar, and an obscure notion told him he should have identified it.

Stifling a yawn, he sat rigidly, listening. Something shrieked piercingly close by. The noise of an animal, a high yelp, which seemed to come from deep within his head, made him question the state of his mind for the first time in his life.

Some form of life had invaded his intellect, was communicating with him.

Allan shook his head to clear it.

Bark! Bark! Bark!

Save for the joyous beating of his heart, the poor man was too worn-out, too dazed to wonder at it. A broad smile spread on his face.

"Matey? Matey, you've come back!" he cried, looking about.

Another bark boomed in the keeper's ear. This time, it had a definite marked edge of impatience.

"What is it, boy?"

A volley of snarls and yelps, urgent and pleading answered him.

An emergency warning! The light! The fog!

Years of training took over. Instantly alert, Allan yanked the rope, three times. Three strikes a minute, that's what was needed.

It was the last dogwatch[4] aboard *The Marilyn*.

"Foghorn at starboard bow!" bellowed the lookout, cocking one ear.

Invisible, the foghorn continued to bray.

[4] Between 6:00 P.M. and 8:00 P.M.

"Ten points off the bow!" shouted the Master after a quick check at the compass. "Fast approaching."

Pale-faced and terrified, all hands seemed to freeze in place.

Eyes riveted on starboard, the captain bellowed as calmly as possible. "Prepare to come about!"[5]

"All hands on deck!" ordered the boatswain at the top of his voice. *The Marilyn* burst into frenzied action. Pandemonium ruled the deck. Men dashed to their posts. The helmsman tensely gripped the helm, waiting for orders. Hands and feet climbed riggings with incredible speed. It was like an army preparing for battle. "Raise the sails! Haul the halyards!"

Suddenly, a hardly discernible yellow light rose through the thick fog.

"Put your helm down! Turn hard to port!" roared the captain between two shallow breaths.

The Marilyn creaked and strained under the helmsman's command and began to turn her bow.

Shouts, frantic voices penetrated the thick layer of ashen mist imprisoning Allan in the tower. He was in a pitiable state of fatigue, sounding the horn incessantly but too weak to work fast. Above the racket of the bell he could hear wild chaos outside. The characteristic moans of wood and straining of riggings told him a schooner was on a collision course with the shoal and light, and struggling to turn about. He listened anxiously to *The Marilyn* groaning close by.

Judging by the quickly approaching bedlam, he figured impact would occur in ten seconds; he crossed himself.

One could never tell what a ship might do.

The impact shook the tower so strongly, the keeper's teeth rattled.

Just as he ran to the door to lend a hand, a furious bark burst in his ears. As Allan would swear later, two strong paws pounded him in the back with such power that he toppled to the floor.

[5] To Turn

Seconds later, *The Marilyn*'s figurehead crashed through the glass and embedded itself into the wall.

Right where Allan had been standing.

Long before the bridge was erected and became a landmark, mariners dreaded going through the Straits of Mackinac and its many hazards.

Underneath shallow waters, sometimes less than twelve feet deep, a dangerous shoal extends several miles into Lake Michigan, a major threat to navigation.

In 1832, a wooden lightship was anchored on the spot to mark the perilous formation. In 1851, it was replaced by a proper light resting on the reef atop a timber crib filled with rocks, the first known of this type of structures on the Great Lakes.

A large pier was added in 1871 and a fog signal in 1883.

The light was decommissioned and abandoned in 1912. Although time and elements have wrought their fury on the conical structure, it still stands. This is particularly surprising since it was used as a target practice during World War II.

The pier has crumbled away, the steel sheeting protecting the tower has gradually fallen into the lake, and the "bird cage" is the only vestige left of the lantern and parapet. The structure threatens to tumble into the depths of the Straits.

During the Great Chicago Fire in 1871, a thick fog of ashes engulfed Lake Michigan for three days, catching navigators unaware and creating havoc; errant and blind vessels collided and sank, men were hurled into the frigid water.

The keeper of Waugoshance, James Davenport, was stranded alone at the station when the inferno began. The station had a rope-operated fog bell that he managed to blast for the whole duration of the disaster by sitting in a chair, pots and pans piled on his lap, the rope tied to one wrist. Every time he fell asleep, his pans tumbled to the floor and woke him up.

Because of his stamina and ingenuity, only seven ships were damaged during the ordeal.

Fort Gratiot Light, 1868
Lake Huron

The Door

"At last, no more complaining about my cooking!" The woman muttered to herself as she shoved the last piece—a foot—of her husband's mutilated body inside the wood stove. Iris stoked it a couple of times before banging the cast-iron door shut. She merrily pranced around, wiping a bloody butcher's knife on her starched apron.

"Food! Food! That's all you thought about, Giles, you old bugger. Before the night's o'er, you'll be hamburger. Peace at last. How lovely!"

She filled a kettle with water and slapped it on the black top. Wiggling her body in a comfy position on a faded horsehair armchair, she sighed with satisfaction. A nice cup of tea, that's what she needed, then off to the tower to light the lantern and keep it going. Not much to it, really, not worth the moans of that cranky old goat. Melt some lard oil, climb eighty-six feet worth of cylindrical stairs, feed it to the lamp, light the wick, and watch a warm glow spread through darkness.

The stove roared.

"Giles, you're going with a blast!"

One hour later, carrying a container of preheated lard in a pot safely hugged to one hip, the new keeper lightheartedly skipped up the winding steps to the lantern, holding fast to the rail.

She poured and poured until all the oil was gone from the container, but somehow the wicks were still dry. Strange. Iris squatted to check for leaks. Nothing. She shrugged her broad shoulders, "Looks like it needs more. Down I go then." She began her descent, humming: ". . . Old Bugger . . . Hamburger . . ." She was far too gleeful to notice a shaft of darkness, dim, deep, a spiral of gloom boring through rock and stone, like a bottomless pit to the center of the earth. It whispered and beckoned with persistent eagerness. It called and drew inexorably.

Panting a little, eyes filmed with rapture, down and down Iris went. She was oblivious to the steps changing from metal to stone so worn and decrepit, as though millions of people had treaded over them for centuries. Over contorted shadows and cracks she followed the insistent murmur until her body collided with a solid greenish door. Her face broke out in joyous curiosity. Look at what she'd discovered: a new door! Incredible what one noticed without that horrible grouch. She should have killed Giles sooner.

She pushed at it. It yielded without a creak. The enticing buzz instantly died. Iris boldly crossed the threshold. The door swung back and sealed the wretched woman with a dreadful thud in a world of complete darkness and deafening silence. It reeked of a peculiar, acrid odor, very much like the caged tigers of the traveling circus she had gawked at, wide-eyed, in childhood, with a thrilling combination of choking dread and compelling fascination.

The smile upon her lips flickered and died. Her first reaction was to flee, yank the portal open; her fingers crept and clawed blindly, crablike, unable to locate a knob, a break.

A total sense of helpless bewilderment fell upon her. For an instant she stood confused, then tried again; she trembled and banged and shouted simultaneously until, voice cracking and knuckles throbbing, she sagged, moaning, against a slimy surface. The only person for miles around had been Giles, and he was dead.

Wheezing heavily, she slowly came to realize that the room, the black hole she'd stumbled upon, was occupied. Her entrance had disturbed some sort of energy, of life, one she had never experienced. The silence became loaded and frightening, it breathed malevolence. There was a monstrous, evil presence—inaudible, invisible, but alive nevertheless, active and waiting.

Iris slumped prostrate on the damp floor. She heard a soft rustle and noticed a pair of iridescent yellow eyes emerging from the obscurity.

"Who's there?" She panted.

The eyes came closer, accompanied by an eerie shuffling. A mixture of malice and hunger glared in the brilliant pupils.

Back glued to a wall, Iris suddenly turned cold and screamed.

Other creatures appeared. Their shapes were indiscernible, but the eyes multiplied.

And advanced.

More of them crept forward, they gathered in groups, slunk and stole near. Trapped like a wild animal, Iris recoiled and whimpered. Something pricked an ankle and clung. She screamed, inhuman sounds of terror, and struck and batted at whatever chewed and sucked. A fiery pain shot through her. She scrambled wildly, blindly; gruesome, inconceivable thoughts raced through her crazed mind. With unreasoning terror Iris crashed against dank cold surfaces, stumbled, rose again, feet and hands clambering over furry, hissing things.

Iris toppled again. Harder.

Dozens of dilated, greedy pupils surrounded her and fixed on her cornered figure.

There was no way out. She rolled into a fetal position.

They leapt forward.

Fort Gratiot Lighthouse is the oldest surviving tower in Michigan and stands in superb condition. The original building was erected in 1825 on Lake Huron, near historic Fort Gratiot, an American outpost established in 1814 to defend the border against an eventual British offensive.

A violent storm destroyed this structure in 1828, but thanks to a certain Lucius Lyon, it resumed service in 1829. The tower was raised to its present eighty-six feet in 1861. In 1874-75 a two-story dwelling was designed and built to house the keeper, his assistant, and their respective families.

It was automated in 1933.

As you may have guessed, no evil spirits lurk in the tower; if you climb the stairs, you will come out alive. Just make sure no deep, dark secret rests on your shoulders . . .

Ile aux Galets (Skillagalee) Lighthouse, 1996
Straits of Mackinac

Friends

"It looks like a storm is forming over there," I said, pointing to the gathering of gray clouds coming our way.

Julie, the friend sharing the boat with me, stopped rowing and lifted her gaze to the darkening sky. She shrugged nonchalantly with the usual disregard for caution that had first captivated me five years ago. "Let's keep going. We'll just shelter in the light." She blew on a stray curl tickling one eye. "Here, take the oar, you're stronger. We might beat it."

We had met during our sophomore year in college. Me, reserved and brooding, unsure of myself, full of my father's stern evangelical dogma, and her—ebullient, joyfully alive and daring—a golden girl. She was freedom, vitality, wind and sky. Julie needed no one, knew no boundaries; she took it all. And I, irresistibly attracted to her world, had offered my poor naive brain to spiritual seduction; previously inconceivable thoughts floated in my mind and sometimes out of my mouth. Free as air, with a wild abandon to sensuality, she thirsted for all kind

133

of people, of lovers. She hovered on the brink of perdition and I recklessly followed, freshly released passion itching for greater heights, for unmentionable carnal exploits.

We became so happy, so liberated in each other's company. We've been close friends ever since.

"How was he?" She'd asked when I returned to our digs after a night with a man. If I replied, "Gorgeous" or "Great," she'd raise one eyebrow. "Serious?" One shake of my head, and an impish grin lifted a corner of her wet lips "Can I try?"

"If he's willing, go ahead."

The same type of date attracted us; so far this had not been a problem. One of us backed off or waited for a turn. I backed off a lot.

Men noticed her first. How could they not? There was an air about her: an unruly mop of crazy blond curls over a pair of sultry eyes darkened by open invitation; a suppleness of movements, of long legs sumptuously encased in silk stockings; an amused tug of the lips. It was the look of a woman challenging men to outdo themselves. The provocation titillated egos, each man foolishly hoping to be the one to end the wandering. I was more discreet, although my rich chestnut hair and hazel eyes attracted their fair share of lovers.

We'd sworn nothing—passion, desire—could mar our relationship, and we'd succeeded. Our best times were spent together.

Two weeks ago we had rented a cottage with frontage on the Straits of Mackinac. A lighthouse sitting on a minuscule island with the quaint French name of Ile aux Galets (Island of Pebbles) was visible from the yard. In the distance, it looked decrepit and abandoned, at least we'd never seen anyone there. Its light did not flash and the tower appeared riddled with gaping holes. Nevertheless, it stood steadfast, a melancholy and mysterious vestige of a bygone era.

"Let's go see it, " Julie had suggested after lunch, slipping inside a sleek pair of shorts and halter, her lithe figure fragrant with tropical sunscreen.

As we rowed toward it, the light looked different, not dilapidated at all. The huge holes were shiny windows, and the crumbling parapet was in fact a newly painted lantern room. At close range, it was bright and immaculate in spite of the untimely darkness of the fast approaching storm. I was a bit baffled, confused by the transformation, but kept rowing. Already a few raindrops began to pitter-patter on the skiff and our warm bodies.

As we neared the shore, I noticed a rusty mooring ring anchored in a savagely eroded dock. Julie popped out to fasten a line to it and scurried across the stony land with the agility of a mountain goat. An agitated flock of gulls squawked furiously amid scrawny weeds.

"Quick, it's going to pour in a minute!" She grabbed my hand and tugged me toward the structure. I followed her up a worn flagstone step. She shoved a shoulder against the door. To my amazement, it opened without a creak.

The room was prematurely dim but cozy; it was not of the sort of decor you see these days—a stone floor partially covered with a homespun rug; deep brown and low ceiling beams; a well-worn sofa with a couple of embroidered antimacassars; by a wood stove, a rocking chair.

A man occupied it, a red muffler loosely wound around his neck. I stopped short at the threshold. He was bent over a walnut table littered with a variety of ancient instruments and charts. One hand was wrapped around a chipped enamel mug. That it was dear to its owner was obvious by the way the man's fingers curved softly around it.

The stove glowed in spite of being midsummer, yet the room was not stuffy or hot. A wonderful aroma of freshly brewed coffee wafted from the pot on the corner of the black top.

I felt transported back to the previous century. He was unaware of our presence and appeared unduly thoughtful. Not totally at ease with barging on people's privacy, an awkward feeling made me quietly step back. Not Julie—she bounced forward. "What an exquisite room! We're sheltering from the storm," she declared by way of an explanation. "Do you mind?"

Startled, he raised his head. Immediately dazzled, both of us held our breath. An intense vitality, a compelling sense of brightness and friendliness shone on his features. Fine lines of dissipation broke on his face as he smiled wryly. That made him even more attractive to us.

Underneath a long inky lock, the most brilliant blue eyes roamed over us, settling first on Julie, then me, back to my friend, and back to me. It was more than a passing glimpse; it peeled layers of clothes, lingered at curves; it could not, would not, fix on one of us. The room instantly shrank. Julie and I exchanged brief meaningful glimpses. Both contained an order to back off. My eyes hardened and refused to dip. For the first time we declared open competition.

A faintly humorous grin lifted a corner of his lips. He sprung up, graceful as a panther, smoothly and quietly, and extended a warm hand. "Ah, the rain!" A certain lost look came over him. "Of course, come in."

We introduced ourselves. He nodded his head toward the sofa. There was something of the beast of prey about him altogether—a very handsome one.

I sat on the edge. Julie plopped herself next to me, long legs artfully displayed to their advantage.

"Coffee?"

Peter, that was his name, seized two mugs from a shelf and filled them from the pot. Julie then undulated languorously around the room, mug in hand, pretending to read titles from leatherbound volumes in a beeswax smelling bookshelf. She peered at yellowed photographs, consciously exhibiting a sensuous figure strumming with lust.

Resting a hip on the walnut table, slim and vibrant, hands stuffed in pockets, Peter waited patiently. He followed every move, grinning, showing his white pointed teeth while she unabashedly explored his domain. She luxuriated in his attention, a barely repressed wolfish gleam sneaking into her piercing pupils. She was a woman of action, of passion, anything to assuage longing. What would she do next?

Peter did not ignore me, *au contraire*, smoldering stares tarried my way also. I moodily sipped my coffee, angrily aware that he desired us both. I stood and walked restlessly about the room. Muffled by thick walls, the rain pounded the lighthouse.

"You won't be leaving soon. Not in this—too dangerous," he said, flashing a quizzical smile at us. We sat back in charged silence in the unceasing obscurity.

Peter filled a lamp with kerosene and applied a match to it. It spread a warm amber glow that eased the atmosphere. Guided by him, we engaged in mundane conversation. Mellowed by the mysterious ambiance, we began to relax and talk with more freedom and intimacy. When he talked, there was a slight mocking tone to his speech, and his eyes played round with us. Once or twice, his gaze narrowed on one of us. I felt he was biding his time. Soon it was dinner time, and we shared a couple of cans of soup.

Then it was close to bedtime. I poked my head outside. The storm had increased in intensity; it flung vicious streams of water over my quickly retreating figure. I wondered if there were two bedrooms, and if one of us would share his.

Peter and Julie were whispering secretively. They abruptly stopped to gaze at me in a peculiar way. Here, it comes, I thought. One moment's inattention, and the choice was made.

Peter sat for a while looking at me, then he leaned forward on his rocking chair, eyes narrowed to a slit. "Well, shall we?" he said seductively—and persuasively.

I raised my eyebrows. "Shall we what?"

"Go upstairs. To the bedroom." Wetted lips, Julie cocked her blond mane provocatively.

Did I understand right?

Reading my expression, she nodded in silent agreement. I looked from one to the other, and burst into uncontrollable laughter. Arms entwined, we went up to bed.

The next morning, the cold woke me. Strange, last night we'd huddled underneath a soft quilt, me in the middle. Without opening my eyes, I stretched contentedly and searched blindly for it. I found nothing except Julie snuggled against my chest, no doubt seeking warmth in her sleep. What a night! My limbs ached pleasantly from extraordinary lovemaking.

It felt particularly chilly on my left. "Peter?" No reply. My hand reached for him and met emptiness. Probably making coffee.

Above us, something, a seagull perhaps, screeched loudly, jerking me fully awake. The sound had been loud, clear, and close by. Befuddled, totally confused, I stared in disbelief at a white bird perched on a half-collapsed parapet against the clear blue sky just above our sluggish forms.

Julie and I were lying on bare stones, a slight breeze rustling through gaping holes in the crumbling walls and the collapsed roof. Leaves and dust from past seasons mingled with yellowed candy wrappers, left over by picnickers.

The cozy room with its glowing stove, the bedroom and marble-topped bedside tables, all had disappeared. Peter had gone as well.

Had they ever existed? I helplessly wondered. A clear picture of Peter shot into my mind. He'd been so alive! But then, a rocking chair near a stove that queerly glowed without heat, a woolen muffler in midsummer . . . No. It could not be; my hands had felt his warmth. The remembrance of the previous night was too real to deny its existence.

We were naked. And alone in a derelict lighthouse. "Julie, wake up!"

She turned languidly my way. "Mmmmmm."

"No, wake up, look around."

Her gaze roamed uncomprehendingly over the ruins. After a while, "And it was so good," was all she said.

We got up and dressed in silence. Without thinking, I glanced at a red muffler lying on a small pile of rubbish swept into a corner by the wind. Suddenly, "My God!" I cried as Julie simultaneously exclaimed, "Eh, what is that?" She picked up a tattered black book and fingered through it.

"Hey, listen! It's a keeper's log. How peculiar! It mentions one keeper, Peter Wayne—that's our Peter's name. It says that he was recalled June 12, 1925 and discharged from service for misconduct and dissipation a year later." She looked puzzled. "I can't imagine why. Can you Mark?"

The light on Ile aux Galets, first named by French explorers and fur traders, has been mispronounced Skilligalee almost from its beginning in 1868. It was built to warn passing ships of the presence of this rather flat island, a very peculiar danger to navigation as the ever-changing water level increases or decreases the spread of the land beside the shipping channel going through the Straits.

Apart from scant shrubs and wind-beaten trees, the island belongs to the birds, especially gulls.

Surrounded by aquamarine water, it offers quite a marvelous sight. The present white tower dates from 1888 and, unlike the one described in the story, is in good condition. To this day a marvelous focal point for professional mariners as well as recreational boaters, it stands fifty-eight feet above the mean low water level of Lake Michigan.

Bete Grise (or Mendota) Light, 1890
Lake Superior

Shining Love

A clock is ticking, the whir of its mechanism as it prepares to strike six o'clock catches Katherine's heartbeat. Its murmur stretches like a cat's purr at the end of a lazy afternoon. A blanket of lead, of autumn gloominess, rolls across the sky; a chill marches into the kitchen, the wind boldly knocks on the door. Six o'clock, six o'clock chimes the regulator in that haven of peace, of salvation, the only house on a solitude of land battered by frigid waters.

The room grows dark.

The woman, that gentle angel of mercy, brings a match to a lantern. She climbs the creaking stairs, glancing up at the window, a thin pane separating her illuminated world from the blackness of loneliness, of solitary sailing, everywhere alone.

Bete Grise Bay, the only refuge for vessels caught in a northerly storm on Lake Superior, lurks by the lee of the Keweenau Peninsula, an inky pool impossible to locate but for the glowing love of a woman. In a voice sunk to a loving whisper, "Come to me, dearest, with this light, I guide thee." She says to her husband, fishing, earning a meager living out in the wet world.

She returns to the kitchen, stokes the stove and peels vegetables for tonight's stew.

All evening the light shines softly upon its sill, a feeble flicker of hope clinging to the shores of the mighty Superior, its waves exploding against the bay. The woman picks up her knitting and sits by the spitting stove.

As the hands of time inexorably pursue their march, the ragout bubbles impatiently. Katherine's own hands fumble with their task; her chest rises and falls. She breathes dread. An occasional tremor runs through the house. The outside world is growing angry; its fury roars overhead and around the house, but inside, it is quiet, so quiet and still!

Katherine moves the pot to a corner of the stove. Then, by the clock and sky, it is deep, dark night. Untouched, untasted, the stew thickens and burns.

The appalling chaos shaking the waters slams against the walls in powerful battering gusts. Katherine hears it, feels it; its full force assaults her heart, her entrails, coiling tightly around faith and hope, squeezing and squeezing.

The ragged breath, the emptiness of fear.

Praying feverishly, "Sweet Mary, Mother of God!" Fingers plucking at her aching heart—for faith and hope keep life pulsing, to lose them both surpasses any losses—she climbs the creaking stairs again. By the flickering light, she peers at the world outside and recoils. Spray beats against the window. She watches mountainous waves lift and twist as though in agony. Such a chasm, so huge, so inconceivable, so close to hell; an upside down world; hell on top, heaven below, heaven that cannot be reached, lost in the abyss, in a black hole of despair.

Does it hurt to die?

Katherine's face turns ghastly white. Her eyes imagine the tortured motions of her husband's boat, the creaking and groaning of planking and masts, the horror, the cries of terror.

Once stupefied with horror, she now seizes the lantern. "Come to me, dearest. With this light I guide thee." She begins her vigil.

Alone in the dark, too cold, too wet, too weary to furl his mangled sails, "I wonder who will miss me most," her husband cries to the gale that snatches his little vessel to another place, to the top of raging water, a peak of fear, despair and hope. Surrounded by reefs and hidden dangers, the difference between life and death, he seeks the light, the one that has guided him back to safety so often before. "Katherine, shine thy love!"

One moment he implores God to grant him life, another he gulps fiery liquor to appease terror, the amber liquid sloshing against his frozen face. A sailor always thirsts for the shore, to die with land in sight surpasses in cruelty any perversion devised by sea demons.

Ghosts—tormented souls gone to God before their time in a gutting of steel and wood, torn from rails, swallowed by raging surf—crouch low over inky water, today, forever. They wait, ready to leap; for, had they a choice, they would rather not have died, and as such wish to unleash their wrath on hapless beings. Their clawlike fingers crawl silently over and under the surface of the lake in a never-ending search, undulating tentacles of doom.

All but Jenny, the All-Seeing One. Concealed in a maze of wood at the bottom of the lake, her long blond hair tangled in the weeds growing in a wreck of long, long ago, she watches. When did her eyes begin to pierce the darkness of the underworld? She does not know. Fifty, a hundred years ago?

She whispers softly to the emptiness in her cradling arms, "Don't worry, Jeremy, I can see your papa. You go back to your sweet sleep." Cocking her head to a world she no longer belongs to, "Paul, Paul, is it you? Do you need help?" she whimpers.

But she knows she is not strong enough. Not yet. Not yet. Not without Paul.

In the eye of the storm, the man feels the spirits' hungry caresses on the belly of his boat, a slight scratching of nails, digging, digging. Visibility is nil. "God, I am in your hands now!" he breathes, and wonders how long before they strike—one minute, two minutes, one hour?

Then tons of water blot everything out.

As it has done so often before, the lake pulls into its depth the collapsing confusion of man, splitting wood, rigging and sails. The demons' fingers pluck wildly at the vessel, at each other, at anything that can feed their eternal hunger, "Give me, give me, give me." Their shapeless mouths open wide to devour morsels of human flesh, to suckle the surface of the lake for blood, the preferred drink of erring souls.

There is another emptiness, colder than winter, beating within Katherine's breast.

"Oh, my dear! No!" She screams in agony, eyes blazing, the ghost of her husband's tormented face peering at her through the glistening window.

Jenny stoops to the bottom of the wreck, gently loosens her arms. "Shush, Jeremy. You wait for Mama," she says, patting the water.

A moment later, as though God himself had tired of Nature's devilish plays, there is a shattering noise; lightning briefly rips the clouds apart, thunder booms through hell. The elements hear

their master's voice, they abate. The demons scatter, crawling and whimpering like chastised dogs.

Jenny surges.

All evening *The Gloria* had blindly fought a welter of raging foam, the Captain seeking the Keweenau Peninsula, the winds remorselessly dragging her toward unknown dangers. Once, the floundering ship had slammed against rocks and every moment the men had expected the gutting of her bottom plates. There was a slight leak on the port side and water slowly seeped in with a horrible gurgling sound.

"The blasted charts," barked the Captain impatiently, "show no buoys, no lighthouse! They say a woman sometimes keeps a light shining for her husband. If only . . . if only . . ."

At last, about midnight, suddenly and for no apparent reason, the storm diminished in an explosion of thunder, so much like an enraged and sinister spirit.

Now, lightning illuminated the night sky in crackling spurts.

"Captain! Captain!" shouted the lookout at the top of his voice, after a brief glimpse of the water. "Man overboard!"

"Wher'-o-way? Wher'-o-way?" came the Captain's voice in the ensuing darkness.

"On our lee-quarter, sir!" Another bolt of lightning.

Sure enough, on a makeshift raft of tangled wood, lay the body of a mangled man where no raft could or ought to have drifted. It was so remarkable, so unnatural that, "Blessed be!" cried a sailor, his whole body rigid with apprehension.

"Where does he come from?" muttered the Captain, shaking his head.

In another instant the raft had floated within a few feet. "Moore and Knight get him!"

A boat was lowered alongside the ship and the sailors hoisted the man into it. The instant he fell in, a frothy wave lifted itself from the surface of the lake and bore away the raft. It disappeared.

A small heaving of the man's chest showed them he was alive.

Moore and Knight later swore they saw webs of yellow and

green strands, almost like snarled hair and weeds, pull the raft to the vast depths of the lake. They claimed the abating wind carried the sound of a woman's voice singing what they described in hushed tones as a sweet, melancholic lullaby.

"In the heavens, it must be Jenny Rafferty!" exclaimed an old mariner, quickly making the sign of the cross. "Has to be her. 'Been erring, waiting for her husband for years. Haven't you seen her or heard her wails before?" Above their heads, thunder and lightning continued their jousting. The crew was silent. "It was in the 1700's," shouted the old man above the fracas. "Their ship sank. In the panic, the couple's baby boy was knocked from his mother's arms into the lake. Jenny wrenched free of her husband's grip, screaming 'Wait for me, Paul!' She plunged after their son. Both disappeared. The husband drowned with the rest of the passengers and crew." For a moment the men experienced that sickening feeling at the pit of their stomach when coming across tragedy.

The Captain, however, casting his eye at the heavens, shouted, "Storm gathering again!"

In the house by the shore, the woman wakes from her trance. She ceases to tremble. "Heavens above, he is safe but lost." She quickly refills the lantern. Arms outstretched, "Come to me, dearest, with this light I guide thee," she pleads.

The light, bursting through the midnight gloom, like some distant and old-fashioned miracle, reaches the leaking ship adrift upon the lake. "Come to me, come to me," it echoes from the tip of Katherine's fluttering hand.

The moaning husband spies it upon the waters borne, sweeter than sunshine on a cold winter's day. "Cherished be the light and blessed be the hand that holds it!" he cries.

"Land-a-ho!" yells the lookout.

Thus guided, the captain boldly steers his stray vessel into the sanctuary of Bete Grise Bay.

At the bottom of the abyss, Jenny, crouched in a corner of her wreck in a solitude of sea, desolately hangs her head. "It was not your papa, Jeremy. We have to keep looking."

For many years mariners had requested that a light be built in Bete Grise Bay to mark the entrance of the Mendota Channel, the narrow passage linking Lac La Belie to Lake Superior. The bay, protected by the Keweenau Peninsula, is the only shelter for vessels caught midway in a storm on Lake Superior. It's also an impossible place to locate in the dark. Finally, in 1895, the Bureau of Lighthouses acquiesced and the light was erected.

Until then, the only light shining in that area was tended by Henrietta Bergh out of her own free will and at her own expense. Her husband was a commercial fisherman; every time he was late coming in off the lake, she placed a glowing kerosene lantern in an upstairs window to guide him back.

Other mariners saw the light or heard of it. Soon, they stopped by her house, and after thanking her for saving their lives, they asked if she could keep the lantern burning every night until dawn. Henrietta agreed.

For years she tended a kerosene lantern specially designed by her husband to last all night, without any governmental compensation. She claimed her reward lay in the appreciation and the smiles of those stopping by.

When the light was finally built, she agreed to become its first keeper. She may also have been the first female lighthouse keeper on Lake Superior.

Point Iroquois Lighthouse, 1982
Lake Superior

Fred, Chuck and Harry

"This lady didn't leave a message but said it was important you called as soon as possible. Sounded kind of excited."

I thanked the earnest young man at the desk and, recognizing the number scribbled on the piece of paper, smiled. Terry—my sister—like a crop of hops, is always fermenting and on the verge of bubbling over.

She answered the phone on the first ring. "Elizabeth? Oh, Elizabeth, am I glad you called! I have found the perfect thing for you!"

Placing the phone one foot away from my ear, "What is it?" I asked wearily. Ever since my retirement as a nurse, three months before, Terry had come up with the most incredible schemes to "keep me busy."

Ignoring my question, she screamed, "When can you leave?" Although she lived at Sault Ste. Marie, near the Soo Locks, her voice rose above the distance to reach Marco Island as clear as a bell—a warning bell.

"Leave? Leave? I've just arrived." I had just escaped a cold

Michigan winter and was not about to give up eight days of sun and Pina Coladas.

"Listen, it's perfect," she continued, unabashed. "You know the lighthouse at Point Iroquois, just near the St. Mary's River? It's available, free of charge, for up to two years!"

Terry and I share the same love for history and old buildings. We had often visited the Point. It is close to her home and the view is magnificent. We'd stand at the water's edge and roll back to 1662, shivering, imagining the cries of an Iroquois war party being ambushed and slaughtered one by one by an army of Ojibway; hence the name of the Point.

The light had illuminated one of the busiest shipping lanes in the world for over a century, especially after the construction of the Soo locks connecting Lake Superior to the other Great Lakes. Ships searching for the entrance of the St. Mary's River face many perils. On one side are the reefs near Gros Cap in Canada, and on the other stand the treacherous rocks of Point Iroquois. A small light was erected in 1857 to help the captains. It was remodeled into a sprawling dwelling with an imposing sixty-five foot tower in 1871. And then, in 1962, after one hundred years of performing its duty flawlessly, the Coast Guard disconnected it in favor of a beacon farther out in the water.

"Are you there?" Impatience sharpened Terry's voice.

"What's the catch?" Free lodging does not come without some string.

"The light now belongs to the National Forest Service. It's been empty for quite a while, and, er, it has not weathered very well." A vision of peeling white paint and sunken ceilings came back to me. My head shook of its own volition.

"They're worried about vandals, insurance liability, the whole gamut. Someone living there would be a deterrent."

Before I could protest, she quickly added, "You're unattached, plenty of free time . . ."

"Terry, I'm not a policewoman. A retired spinster hardly qualifies."

"If no one takes the job, they'll tear it down, there's no other option." That hurt!

"Come on, Elizabeth, you remodeled your old house."

"Yeah. And I just sold the old place to buy a modern condo as soon as possible."

Terry took an audible deep breath. "Anyway, I called them." Pause, followed by a cough. "I sent them your resume. They're interested in your candidacy."

"What?" My voice exploded in the room.

"Next Wednesday, 3:00 P.M. at the light. Be there."

Two months later, in early spring, I was moving to the Point. Day after day, I scraped, plastered and hammered, and as I peeled more and more layers of faded wallpaper, the old girl appeared to me in her original beauty.

In its heyday, a head keeper, two assistant keepers and their families had filled all the spacious living space at the station and a school had been established for their offspring. In fact, the Point had become so jolly that it turned into an unofficial meeting place for the locals. Children's laughter echoed in my ears; men and women strolled in my mind.

How I loved the old girl! Kissed by the sun and spray, stroked by early morning mist, stung by the wind. All her moods had become my companions.

As spring turned into summer, as their predecessors had done many decades ago, some of the locals dropped by to check on the renovation progress or just to have a chat. My favorites were three men, whose last names and occupations I never knew, but who went by the names of Fred, Chuck and Harry and lived together in a shack on the edge of town.

When not waving from their motorboat bouncing on Lake Superior, the threesome walked about the Point, slugging beer and chewing tobacco, always keeping a vigilant eye on the lake and the sky. Fishing almost every day, their moods varied with the spitting of the waves, the burst of dark clouds and the catch of the day. They brightened my days with the atmosphere of good humor they diffused. "The mighty Superior," Harry would say, gazing at the shoreline, "it ain't a friend."

August arrived, and a subtle change came over Harry. I could not have said what, maybe a slight shudder as he studied the lake, the fading of his color or the deepening of the hollows under his eyes. Once he mumbled, "Has such an eye on me," and I sensed a queer weight of fatigue falling upon him. His fingers bit into my arms and then there was that pleading look in his eyes. "You ought to be careful, you know. It is waiting."

So far, the lake had been playful, rolling its varicolored waves on the rocks and I had enjoyed its chilly spray on my face, but now Harry's words changed all that. Behind its foamy crests, one sensed mischief, a mighty force waiting to unleash its power; in the midst of its cold water lay an icy grip. Had my body not felt on more than one occasion an almost unnoticeable tug toward the water's edge, a sort of a magnetic pull toward a greater depth? In its abyss, the lake had a soul with dark edges, its all-seeing mind conspired to feed its eternal hunger.

Now, its call pounded in my ears. I barely kept from crying out, from losing my hold and slipping down into the fathomless blackness that beckoned me. Blocking the sound with trembling hands, I screamed thinly and whirled to run on wobbly legs. Run, run, run anywhere from that ghastly place. I burst into the house and bolted the door. By then, I was almost convinced that I was going mad, but the part of my brain, where logic lay, rejected the thought.

Like a frightened child, I sought more and more the protection of my old girl, that silent, steadfast soldier standing between me and an indescribable danger.

Fall came, the light was almost ready for its official reopening the next season, when the National Forest Service expected me to guide visitors through it. The leaves turned to gold and the lake began to grumble and roar and bite at the shoreline, brushing it with teeth of steel. Like an animal before hibernation, it angrily sought its final dinner. Its moans haunted my nights.

Impervious to the menace—I began to wonder if the threat was directed only at Harry and me—Fred and Chuck happily bounced on the swollen crests, blowing their horn on the way in, casting their lines on the gray water, wiping twirling sleet off their faces. But Harry, oh Harry was different. His smile was ghastly and his face had become prematurely lined and gray.

One morning in late fall, I woke to indifferent weather, the sort that has not yet decided to go for a last fling of balmy sun rays or for a preview of things to come. Fred and Chuck waved as usual, their craft plunging over bulging water, their heads snugly ensconced in bright orange foul-weather gear, fishing rods poking at the sky. A sickly smile hung about Harry's lips.

Then I noticed the lake. It was different from any mood it had dared show so far. Its spray burst into leers; a strange mix of greed and anticipated contentment rode its waves. The discovery sent a cold current through my limbs; a dreadful sense of mortal isolation sank into my heart. Cupping my hands around my mouth, I shouted and screamed for Fred, Chuck and Harry to return. The wind, fiendish traitor, only smiled and carried my cries the other way.

The afternoon turned into a whipping, snarling day; no craft went by and no horn blew, I dusted furniture that had no dust and polished untarnished silver, my favorite opera blasting over the booming waves. Now and then, my eyes glanced furtively out the window.

I tried to settle in my old armchair by the wood stove to brush up on the history of my dwelling with an old copy of *Lighthouse Memories* by Betty Byrnes Bacon, whose father had been head keeper in the 1920s. My eyes kept searching the horizon framed by flowery drapes; my breathing became more shallow, my chest constricted.

An hour or two went by. Freezing, howling spray began to pound on the walls of the house. "I hear you! I hear you!" My lips shouted at the raging water.

Someone screamed—a bloodcurdling cry of utter terror. Startled, I spun toward the sound—the window—and stared hard at the face of my enemy, for that's what the lake had become. Suddenly, there on the water, shot a hundred feet away before me a wild light, and a small, dark shape poked through the deluge. Three orange-clad men—only later would the clarity of the sight strike me as queer—turned twisted, sad faces at me, waving bloody, mangled arms as in parting, their little craft surfing the high crest as if on clouds. I longed to reach out, to touch them, but somehow knew that if I did the sight would disappear and never return. The lake exploded into a thunderous roar, foam splashed on the pane, blocking my sight for a few seconds.

"Fred! Chuck! Harry!" I screamed, bolting through the door.

Outside I stood stupefied with horror by the ghastly spectacle. An ethereal red cloud surrounded the three men. Agonizing wails rode the wind. Veins pulsing with terror, I dropped on my knees to pray for help, for salvation, for relief. My eyes closed against the sight.

When I opened them, the men, the boat, had disappeared. And the lake, as if suddenly magically appeased, was retreating, its mood had changed to malevolent triumph. In the darkest of nights I saw its steely teeth gleaming and heard the satisfied belch of its swollen belly. Somehow, as never before, I knew.

Fred! Chuck! Harry!

I hurried up to my old girl and fumbled with the door. Gradually the tumult in my brain subsided. Had I been victim of hallucinations? What about calling the police? How futile that would be! "Officer, I had a vision . . ."

Several days later, Lake Superior regurgitated its victims; the bodies of the three men were found, bashing against the reefs of Gros Cap.

For weeks after, as I mourned my companions, every time a board creaked in my old girl or a wave crashed on the shoreline, I cringed. On a cold November day, I moved out and have never been near a lake since.

Although the setting is real and the history of the lighthouse factual, this story is mostly fictitious. An anecdote told to me by a charming elderly lady who lived two years at Point Iroquois lighthouse, over dinner at a Great Lakes Lighthouse Keepers conference on Beaver island, triggered my imagination.

Point Iroquois Lighthouse's extensive building and impressive 65-foot tower are now used as a museum and bookstore and can be toured from Memorial Day through October 15. Betty Byrnes Bacon's book is on sale there. Call (906) 437-5272 for more information.

Lonely Island, 1880
Near Manitoulin Island, Canada

Glorious Health

I should have felt terrible.
I felt terrific.

Underneath my hand, laying with sleepy abandon on my chest, my heart pumped strongly; each beat spread a lazy contentment through limbs and mind. I could not bear to open my eyes. Not yet. Not yet. Such bliss, such health had not pulsed through my body for weeks.

A warm sunray, the first of the year, had gently woken me up. Spring had come at last. The thought brought a sigh of relief to my lips. Winter had been so very, very long, as cruel and merciless as a starving beast.

A sudden hoarse bark exploded in my ear. A wet nose sniffed and blew on my face, a warm tongue washed me thoroughly. Shep!

"So, you made it too, old boy," I said gleefully, scratching a floppy ear. He too appeared in excellent shape, shiny coat and plump belly.

I was too lost with joy to pay attention to our surroundings.

155

Last year, at the end of the shipping season, my assistant had begged me to leave Lonely Island to rejoin the mainland for winter, but I had no family, no pressing matter awaiting me. I had decided to stay here weeks earlier. Dried and canned food lined my pantry, salted fish hung in the icehouse, and huge, neat piles of chopped wood rested sturdily against the exterior walls of my dwelling. Many books and heavy layers of writing paper lay untouched in trunks, especially amassed until the moment when the steamer had whistled its goodbye with my assistant on board, and time was my own.

"Master Kinnon, you'll die if you remain here! Winter is horrid!" Poor Henry had begged me to change my mind.

"Nobody has ever survived winter on the island. Leave!" I just shook my head.

My resolution was irrevocable; nature and its endless challenges had always appealed to me. I viewed a winter alone with Shep on Lonely Island, which well deserved its name, as the ultimate test to my skills.

Henry gone, no battering storm, howling wind and crashing waves had upset my confidence. Ice held the island within a tight grip, my roof creaked and moaned under a heavy layer of snow. Shep and I bore the elements' assaults steadfastly and smugly.

All went well until February. In spite of strict rationing, the fireplace had gobbled up the last cord of wood—a grave miscalculation on my part. I trudged daily, wind howling in my ear, snow up to my thighs, scrounging for whatever debris I could burn.

Then, one evening, fate dealt a mighty blow.

Huddled under a warm blanket in a wobbly chair drawn close to a meager fire, Shep at my feet, I was puffing on a well-worn pipe. Such was the irony that I had stocked enough tobacco but not enough wood. Suddenly a violent fit of coughing stole my breath away. I whizzed and spat for what seemed an eternity. When the crisis ended, I stared at my blood-red kerchief with dismay and fear. All symptoms pointed to one malady: consumption. My mother had gone that way.

Cut off from the rest of the world without a doctor and medication, the isolation of the place began to press upon me; survival would summon all of my will and a fair amount of grace from God. Survive I would; never had determination been firmer to beat a disease that ate my dream, if only to show Henry it could be done.

Two weeks later, quivering feverishly, my body as limp as a rag, I dragged a mattress to the chimney where the last of a small pile of twigs and scraps crackled and spat feebly. Then there was no more; I was too sick to stumble in the snow and no shelf, no inside door or furniture was left to burn.

Shep and I curled up underneath several blankets in the icy chill of the room, dragging our weakened bodies out of bed only to open cans of frigid food. Each repulsive bite brought searing pain to my heaving chest, but I forced it down for I kept on fighting and fighting; each thin cold stream of breath coming out of my frozen lips told me to hang on. To stare young Henry in the face, "You see, I survived winter!" was all that mattered.

Soon, as I ebbed in and out of consciousness, days blended into nights.

I have no recollection of the events leading to my recovery. The sound of voices outside jerked me out of my reverie. I scrambled up and for the first time looked about me. We were in the lantern room. How odd! I could not explain what I was doing here or how I came to it.

Frowning, I crossed the floor to peer out of the surrounding windows. There was a good view over my house and the lake. Most of the snow had melted; waves nibbled at the shore. A ship was anchored a little away and a large rowing boat swayed gently by the dock. I could see people running, agitated. Probably looking for me, I thought. Better hurry. But there was something sinister about their demeanor.

Somewhere somebody called; a cry burst from somewhere in my abode. A feeling of strangeness seeped into me.

I heard footsteps coming up the steel steps. The door opened. A man appeared in its aperture. There was a little pause when he saw me.

"Hello, glad to see you." I said cheerfully.

He obviously did not share my feelings because a nameless fear creased his face into a thousand lines. He screamed and fled, his boots thudding frantically down the tower.

Astonished, I stared, confused, at the empty doorway. "Come on, Shep, let's go."

Shep shook his back and padded ahead down the stairs. Outside, he sniffed at a patch of brown grass and cocked his leg.

"Hey, you!" I shouted to the back of a sailor coming out of an outdoor building. He turned around with an expression in his eyes that chilled me. The frightened man bolted away as if a demon was after him.

The full strangeness of it all began to hit me. It was I! People were afraid of me! There must be something wrong with me, something I could not see. I scrambled furtively down the rickety one hundred wooden steps leading to the water's edge, Shep by my side. Crouching there beside the water, I peered nervously into it. My reflection wavered a bit at me; all was normal, it was the face I had shaved for many years. The familiar sight did not reassure me, on the contrary.

A figure I knew well was walking gloomily from my house to the dock with a large canvas bag slung over one shoulder. "Henry!" I called and began to stride toward him. "I am alive. Alive!"

"Aaaaah . . . get away! Get away!" the poor fellow croaked, shaking like a leaf, a finger madly pointing at my home.

What was in my house to cause such distress? Suddenly overwhelming terror hit me—my body took possession; it was my turn to run.

At the entrance, I paused. The door was ajar, muted voices reached my ears. I stood there, staring at the handle, too afraid to take it in my hand.

Blood drumming in my veins, I peered through the opening. Close to the chimney, my emaciated figure lay curled on an old mattress, one arm stretched rigidly over Shep's cold body.

We were both dead.

Built in 1870 on the summit of the north bluff of Lonely Island, the square wooden building attached to the keeper's dwelling burnt to cinders and was rebuilt in 1907-8. A new bungalow was added in the 1960's. All that is left of these lovely buildings is the squat second tower (1907); the rest was destroyed in 1995.

Much history and lore are attached to the place. There is an old Indian burial ground beyond where the light used to stand; Indians would stop to talk to keepers but never stepped on the land, regarding it as sacred ground. Once, a keeper decided to spend winter on the island with his dog. Both died of starvation and illness and are buried behind what used to be the oil shed. In 1882, a terrifying hurricane sank *The Asia*. Many bodies washed up on the shore of the island which, people say, became their graveyard. To top it all, the Massasauga rattlesnake, a protected species in Ontario, has called it home for decades.

Bibliography

Briggs-Bunting, Jane. *Laddie of the Light*. Black River Trading Co., Oxford, MI.

Clifford, Mary Louise. *Women Who Kept the Lights*. Cypress Communications, Williamsburg, VA.

Coote, John O., ed. *The Sea*. W.W. Norton and Co., New York, NY.

Gibbons, Gail. *Beacons of Light*. William Morrow. New York, NY.

Great Lakes Lighthouse Keepers Association. *The Beacon* (bi-monthly magazine). Dearborn, MI.

Great Lakes Lighthouse Keepers Association. *Instructions to Lightkeepers*. Dearborn, MI.

Gutsche, Chisholm, and Floren. *Alone in the Dark*. Lynx Images, Toronto, ONT.

Holland, F. Ross. *Lighthouses*. Barnes and Noble Books, New York, NY.

Hyde, Charles. *The Northern Lights*. Wayne State University Press, Detroit, MI.

Lighthouse Digest Magazine. Wells, ME.

Oleszewski, Wes. *Great Lakes Lighthouses*. Avery Color Studios, Marquette, MI.

Olli, Bette McCormick. *The Way It Was: Memories of My Childhood at Grand Traverse Lighthouse*. Lighthouse Publications, Worthport, MI.

Parker, Tony. *Lighthouse*. Hutchingson and Co., Ltd, London, England.

Penrod, John. *Michigan Lighthouses*. Penrod/Hiawatha Co., New York, NY.

Penrose and Penrose. *A Traveler's Guide to 100 Eastern Great Lakes Lighthouses*. Friede Publications, Davison, MI.

Penrose and Penrose. *A Traveler's Guide to 116 Michigan Lighthouses*. Friede Publications, Davison, MI.

Penrose and Penrose. *A Traveler's Guide to 116 Western Great Lakes Lighthouses*. Friede Publications, Davison, MI.

Ratigan, William. *Great Lakes Shipwrecks and Survivals*. Eerdman's Publishing Co., Grand Rapids, MI.

Roberts, Bruce and Ray Jones. *Eastern Great Lakes Lighthouses*. Globe Pequot Press, Old Saybrook, CT.

Roberts, Bruce and Ray Jones. *Western Great Lakes Lighthouses*. Globe Pequot Press, Old Saybrook, CT.

Wagner, John. *Michigan Lighthouses: An Aerial Photographic Perspective*. Wagner Publications. Manistique, MI.

Whiting, J.D. *Storm Fighters*. Bobbs-Merrill Co., Indianapolis, IN.

Williams, Elizabeth Whitney. *A Child of the Sea*. Distributed by the Beaver Island Historical Society, Beaver Island, MI.

Other Books by Annick Hivert-Carthew:

Cadillac and the Dawn of Detroit, Wilderness Adventure Books, 1994
The Bells of Chartres, Trojan Press, 1992
Marie-Therese Guyon Cadillac (audio cassette), Trojan Press, 1993
French Cadillac Biography, XYZ Publications, 1996

Index

A

The Asia 159

B

Beers, Philo 66
Bergh, Henrietta 148
Bete Grise 141, 148
Brown, Chief Lt. Ed
   58

C

Champlain, Samuel de
   25
Colfax, Harriet 46, 50
Crisp Point Historical
   Society 112
Crisp Point Lighthouse
   111, 112

D

Davenport, James 127
Detroit River 105
Donahue, James 16
Douglas, Thomas 25

F

Fort Gratiot Lighthouse
   132
Fort Ontario 58

G

The George Cox 104
Grand Traverse
   Lighthouse 59,
   65
Grosse Ile Historical
   Society 110
Grosse Ile North
   Channel Light
   105, 110

H

Hartwell, Ann 46, 50
Hoar, John 7
Hope Island 1, 7

I

Ile aux Galets 139
Irving, David 58
Isle Royale 104

K

Kirst, Sean 58

L

Lake Erie 27, 37, 105
Lake Huron
   85, 113, 129, 155
Lake Michigan
   9, 43, 59, 67, 121, 133
Lake Ontario
   1, 17, 25, 51
Lake Superior
   95, 111, 141, 149
Leelanau State Park 65
Lonely Island 155, 159
Lorrain Light 27, 35
Lyon, Lucius 132

M

Manitou Island 77, 83
Marblehead Light 37,
   42
Marchildon, Achille 7
Mendota 141, 148
Mendota Channel 148
Michigan City Light-
   house 43, 50

N

New Presque Isle 94
Nottawasaga Island
   Light 113, 120

O

Old Presque Isle Light
   85, 94
Oswego West Pierhead
   Light 51, 58

P

Point Iroquois Light-
   house 149, 154
Presque Isle 94

R

Rock of Ages 95, 104
Ruff, Fred 58

S

Saint Martin Island
   Light 67, 76
Salmon River 25
Selkirk Light 17, 25
Skilligalee 139
Soldenski, John 104
South Haven Light
   9, 16
Strang, James 66

W

Waugoshance 121, 127